THE GALACTIC MI TEAM.

Captain Joshua Price—commanding officer, undercover operative, anthropologist. He didn't always like what the MI team had to do to find the answers his superiors wanted—but he knew how to get them ... no matter what the cost.

Lt. Emma Coollege—call her "Jackknife." Resourceful, fearless, a born survivor. She's the team's on-the-spot expert at everything from weapons to disguises. She's willing to break every rule in the book to get the job done—and she always gets the job done.

Master Sgt. Rocky Stone—tough and deadly, a career soldier. He volunteered for a combat unit so he could be where the action was. But when he found out about Galactic MI, he switched—to get into the real action.

And featuring—

Lt. Rachel Susan Monier—her dossier describes her as a "Long Distance Data Processor." In reality, she's a telepath. With little previous military experience, her remarkable abilities place her at the center of Earth's battle for space dominion.

GALACTIC MI
THE CITADEL

KEVIN RANDLE

ACE BOOKS, NEW YORK

This book is an Ace original edition,
and has never been previously published.

THE CITADEL

An Ace Book / published by arrangement with
the author

PRINTING HISTORY
Ace edition / May 1994

All rights reserved.
Copyright © 1994 by Kevin Randle.
Cover art by Donato.
This book may not be reproduced in whole
or in part, by mimeograph or any other means,
without permission. For information address:
The Berkley Publishing Group,
200 Madison Avenue,
New York, NY 10016.

ISBN: 0-441-00056-8

ACE®
Ace Books are published by The Berkley Publishing Group,
200 Madison Avenue, New York, New York 10016.
ACE and the "A" design are trademarks
belonging to Charter Communications, Inc.

PRINTED IN THE UNITED STATES OF AMERICA

10 9 8 7 6 5 4 3 2 1

PROLOGUE

"This," said the Colonel, "is our enemy."

He pointed at the holographic orb that hovered over the conference-room table. It was a large ship that they had captured a few weeks before. "We know next to nothing about them," he continued, "except they are the only other living spacefaring race we have encountered."

Captain Joshua Price, known as Tree to his friends, wasn't sure the Colonel was right about using the term *enemy*. Price had been on the ship, a huge asteroid that had been converted into a ship by encasing it in metal and adding engines to it. As they had tried to explore it, Price and his team had been captured by it and held for testing. Of course, that was a little strong. The ship had been like a giant rat trap, letting them enter but then sealing itself so they couldn't escape. There didn't seem to be a hostile intent behind it. A yearning for knowledge, a way of exploring the galaxy using a device that was ingenious because it was not faster-than-light, but was fully automated. That seemed to be the key.

There hadn't been a biological entity on board for the purposes of regulating the testing or even designing the testing. There had been no creature on board to handle any of those problems. But there had been one to repair the machinery if it broke down. It had been held in stasis until its special skills had been needed.

Price didn't want to be in the conference room or to listen to the Colonel's briefing. He knew more about the internal workings of the "enemy" craft, of the living, intelligent creature found on board, of the whole system as anyone in the fleet. Hell, the Colonel was reading from a report that Price had helped construct.

"We believe," said the Colonel, "based on what we've been able to learn from the computer systems and records, that the asteroid, the ship, came from a point very near the galactic center."

Price closed his eyes and wanted to scream. This was as boring as anything he'd ever had to do. The Colonel was filling the staff in on what was known and Price already knew it. There were a dozen things he'd rather be doing. He turned slightly and glanced at windows, thick blocks of glass that looked out on the blackness of space. The closest stars were light-years away. Some were very bright, like Venus when it was near Earth. Others were tiny points of dim light almost invisible in the thick haze of drifting hydrogen atoms and space dust.

The Colonel studied the faces of the officers around the table and saw that they were bored. They had heard it all before, seen it all before, and there was nothing new. It seemed to be a staff meeting called simply for the sake of having a staff meeting.

The Colonel grinned and touched one of the buttons in front of him. The orb vanished in a flickering of light. An outline of an alien body appeared, filled in, and then turned at the same speed that the orb had revolved earlier. It gave everyone at the table a complete view of the alien.

It was a small creature with long hair from the elbows to the wrists and from the knees to the ankles. It was feline-looking, with pointed ears and yellow eyes. Of course Price didn't have to see the holo of it. He'd seen it when it first appeared on the alien ship and then had worked with it as they tried to construct common ground for his interrogation of it.

As he watched it rotate above the table, Price thought that it didn't look like much of an enemy. There had only been one of them on the ship and it seemed to function as a maintenance man. It fixed the things that the computer programs and the self-repairing machines couldn't. Just one being that slept through most of the voyage and awakened when something on the ship broke down. At the moment there was absolutely no reason to call it the enemy.

"The autopsy," said the Colonel, "revealed a very simplified internal structure. It looked as if someone had taken the human body, figured the best way to restructure it, and then genetically engineered it to a specific function. One adapted to the function that it fulfilled . . . that is, sleeping most of the time."

Price hadn't been listening closely. He'd been wondering how soon he could get out of the meeting. There were things that he wanted to do. People he wanted to see. And then the Colonel's words sunk in.

"Autopsy?" said Price, not realizing that he had spoken out loud.

The Colonel turned his attention on Price, seemed to pin him to the chair with his gaze. He stared at Price for a full thirty seconds and then nodded. "Yes, autopsy. I'm afraid that the creature died two days ago."

Price was going to protest, to suggest that it had been healthy enough the last time he'd seen it, and then decided to say nothing. He was not an exobiologist, knew next to nothing about the study of anatomy, and didn't know how to begin. Even with that, it didn't seem right that the alien should have died with no warning.

"Dr. James?" said the Colonel.

James stood up. He was a short man with pasty white skin and jet-black hair. There were black circles under his eyes and he had thin lips that made his face look skull-like. His hands shook, as if he didn't like the idea of speaking to the group of officers assembled.

He opened a folder, took a sheet of paper from it, and placed it on the table in front of him. He glanced at it, looked up at the holo, and said, "I have made a detailed study of the internal organization of the specimen . . ."

Price watched the doctor rather than listened to him. He was standing with his hands behind his back, rocking from heel to toe, speaking in a monotone that put generations of medical students to sleep, and giving his information in such detail with so many technical terms that no one other than another doctor would understand it. If he could stay awake long enough to hear much of it.

James wound down and the Colonel took over again. He left the holo of the alien spinning slowly above the table, talking around the problem, letting the ship's chief navigator speak, letting the astronomer speak, and adding his own comments after each.

Finally, when he had dragged it out as long as possible, the Colonel touched a button and the alien vanished. He dropped back into his chair, turned so that he was staring into space, and said, "A spacefaring race we don't know is a danger to us all. They may know exactly where we are but we can only guess where their home world is."

He paused dramatically and then said, "That is why we have been given a new mission. Find them and find out about them and, if necessary, destroy them."

CHAPTER

1

The intelligence office was a small cabin on the main deck of the flagship. It was one of the few with a hatch that could be locked because of the nature of the work. When Price arrived and centered himself, the hatch irised open without his having to use the combination.

Sitting at the console, her back to him, was Lieutenant Emma Coollege, known as Jackknife. She was looking up at a display screen, her fingers on a keyboard. The information parading across the screen was easily visible from the hatch.

"If you're reviewing classified data," said Price, "the hatch should be locked."

She glanced over her shoulder at him. She was a tall, slender woman with delicate features and short blonde hair, the result of a recent assignment. She was as deadly as any member of the team yet looked sweetly innocent. It was the best disguise she could have.

"I know the security regulations as well as you, Tree. I don't have to be reminded."

Price stepped deeper into the office and let the hatch iris shut. He stood looking at the array of screens attached to the bulkhead.

The smaller satellite screens were dark. Only the center screen was being used.

He dropped into the chair next to Coollege and twisted around so that he could watch as she worked. Finally he asked, "Is that anything important?"

"No. Idle curiosity," she said. She let her fingers fall from the keyboard and looked at him. "I was trying to figure out the most likely candidates for the home world . . . Is there something wrong?"

"We lost our major asset."

For a moment she was confused and then said, "What happened? He escape?"

"After a fashion. He died. I just heard the results of the autopsy."

Coollege fell silent and then put her hands back on the keyboard. She cleared the data from the screen, thought for a moment, and then tried to access the new data. She couldn't find it on the menu, and tried to access security files from the flag area. When that failed, she tried the medical section, science section, and finally the intell section though she knew that they had added nothing to it. Access to the intell section was strictly limited to only a few people and it seemed logical that someone else who had that access might have added the data in there.

"I find nothing here," she said.

Price had been watching. "The doctor might not have his notes input yet . . . or it might be under the captain's log or in the regimental commander's private logs."

"Uh-huh." She thought for a moment, glancing up at the top of the bulkhead as she concentrated, and then began to type again. When the security screen flashed, she only grinned, shot a quick glance at Price, and typed in a six-digit code.

"Where in the hell did you get that?"

Still grinning, she said, "I'm in intelligence and part of my job is to know these things."

The menu came up and she began to scroll through it. "Might be here."

The screen showed a coded document labeled simply "Alien Harvest."

She opened the document and saw that it was nothing more

than a report to higher headquarters detailing the finding on the alien ship, including pictures of the equipment found, the interior of the ship, and a brief look at the power plant. It suggested where detailed information could be found under various tabs in the supporting documentation.

"Hell of a lot of work went into that," said Price.

"Nothing about the alien being."

Price leaned back in his chair and rubbed his chin. He realized that he was going to have to shave soon. As a teenager he couldn't wait for his beard to form. Now it was becoming coarser, darker, and the chore of shaving was beginning to annoy him. He thought about having it permanently removed but hesitated. There were still areas where beards were worn and to fit into the local population he needed to be able to grow his own.

"There is something fishy about this," said Price. "I don't like it."

"Why? Because you weren't told that the being had died?"

"That's part of it. We should have been informed immediately. And I should have been at the autopsy."

Coollege shook her head. "You ever been to one of these autopsies?"

"Hell, this wasn't a human. Nothing to get squeamish about. I would have liked to watch just to make sure that everything was done according to the book."

Coollege laughed. "Talk about your intelligence officer getting paranoid. What in the hell are you thinking?"

"Nothing," said Price. "I just don't like relying on information supplied by others when I haven't seen the source of that information."

"I'm sure the doctor was qualified," said Coollege.

"Yeah," said Price.

Coollege turned her attention to the screen and then the keyboard. She closed the files and returned to the main menu. "I don't know where to look for the data."

"Well, we're authorized to see it, so I guess I'll ask the chief of staff where it's hidden."

"Today?"

"No," said Price. "It's too late for us to do anything constructive anyway. Tomorrow. At which time I'll brief both you and Rocky on the next mission."

"Let me guess," said Coollege. "We're going to make a concentrated effort to locate the alien's home world."

"How'd you know?"

"Just makes sense. We find an alien intelligence out there and the first thing we're going to want to do is learn where their home world is located."

Price didn't respond for a moment, thinking. There was nothing else he could say. The briefing in the morning would cover the mission and until that time there was nothing more to discuss.

Finally he said, "You interested in getting something to eat?"

"You know, Tree, that is the one thing we seem to do all the time. Work awhile and then you want to get something to eat."

"Is that a no?"

"It's merely a comment on the situation. It's more of a 'just a minute and let me get ready.' "

"Shut down the computer and lock up," he said, "and I'll meet you in the corridor."

"Right."

Rachel Susan Monier stood at the hatch on the shuttle deck, waiting for it to cycle open. She had just arrived on the shuttle, having come by courier ship from Earth. She had been told that she would be met. No one had met her, other than to place her on the shuttle. Now she stood at the hatch, her small duffel bag in one hand and her computer in the other. But no one had told her a thing other than billeting would be found outside the shuttle bay, that the regimental office was located near the bridge, and that she was now on her own. They were too busy to have someone take her up there.

Of course she hadn't needed the advice of those others about the locations of the billeting cabin or the regimental office. Even though no one had briefed her on it, she knew where they were. Just as she had known that no one would meet her at the shuttle bay or that the mission coming up would move them all from the explored section of the galaxy into an area where only a few scout ships had ever ventured and from which none had ever returned.

The hatch irised open and Monier stepped through into a dimly lighted corridor. Only a few people were walking along it and none of them looked as if they wanted a thing to do with her. They didn't even seem to see her.

She was wearing the uniform of a first lieutenant, though the rank was more honorary than real. She was a short woman, thin with jet-black hair and large brown eyes. There was nothing unusual to distinguish her from any of the others in the corridor.

Without asking directions, she walked aft, studying the corridor. She reached a lift, waited, and then took it to the main deck. She exited, walked down a corridor that was brightly lighted and filled with people doing their jobs. She found the regimental office and entered.

In all the videos and holos she had ever watched, the new man reported in saluting. She stepped to the desk, glanced at the man sitting behind it, tried to salute, and said, "Lieutenant Monier reporting in." She dropped her hand.

The man kept working for a moment and then slowly looked up at her. "First, you don't report to me. Second, you outrank me so there is no need to salute. And third, I'm a sergeant. You never salute a sergeant."

"Sorry . . ."

"Orders," said the sergeant gruffly.

Monier set her duffel on the deck, shuffled through it, and held out the computer disk. The Sergeant tapped the desk on the right with his index finger and let her set it there. He didn't pick it up right away, but closed out the document he had been using.

"You reporting in?" he asked.

"Yes, sir."

That stopped him again. He looked up at Monier, at the silver bar on her collar, and asked, "How long you been in the service?"

Monier focused her attention and began to understand. She smiled and said, "Long enough, Sergeant. I'm just overly polite to my elders. Now please do your job and let the Colonel know that I have arrived."

"Yes, ma'am." He picked up the disk, shoved it into the disk drive, and watched as the screen lit. He read the information, scrolled down, and then laughed.

"I was right," he said. "You were called to active duty just three months ago."

"That's right, Sergeant, but I'm a very fast learner."

He scanned more of the information and asked, "Just what is a Long Distance Data Processor? Sounds like something that should be part of the computer."

One of the few things that she had learned was to say as little about her job as she could. There were those with the need to know and those with none. "It means that I work with computers," she lied.

"Oh."

She stood watching as the Sergeant added her to the computer data base, checked on the authorization codes embedded on the disk, and then removed it from the drive. He held it out. "Here you go. I think before you meet the Colonel you should meet Captain Price. He'll be your boss."

"Price," she said.

"Nice fellow."

"Okay," said Monier. She stuffed the disk into her pocket. "Thanks."

"You go out the hatch, take the mid-lift down two stations. Intell office will be on the right. There is no sign on the door. That's how you know it's the intell office. Everything else is labeled."

"Thanks," she said again.

She left the regimental office and walked to the lift. She rode it down and saw Price leaving the office. Without being told, she knew the officer was Price.

"Captain?"

"Yes."

"Good afternoon, sir. I'm Rachel Monier. I've been assigned to your office."

"Nope," said Price. "I've heard nothing about it."

"You will, sir."

Price waited until Coollege joined them and said, "You know Lieutenant Coollege?"

"Called Jackknife," said Monier.

"Right," said Price.

"You've been doing your homework," said Coollege suspiciously.

Price stood still for a moment and then said, "You want to join us? We're going to get something to eat."

Monier looked at Coollege and then at Price. "No," she said. "I think that I should get settled in first. Find my billet." That was a word she remembered someone using to describe the cabin she would use.

"If you are truly assigned to us," said Price, "then this would be a very good chance for us to get to know one another before we start in the morning."

"I believe . . ." started Monier.

"Join us," said Price. He turned to Coollege. "No reason for her not to join us is there?"

"Nope, Tree. None at all." Her voice had a sharp edge to it that Price ignored.

"Then it's settled."

"I need a place for my duffel."

Price waved at the hatch. "Drop it in there and we'll lock up."

"Yes, sir."

As Monier stepped around him, Coollege leaned close and said, "I thought it was just going to be you and me tonight, Tree. I wasn't counting on reinforcements."

"She's new and is assigned to us."

"So she says."

Monier tossed her duffel through the open hatch and straightened. She was smiling broadly. "I'm ready."

"So are we," said Coollege.

CHAPTER

Randly Clark enjoyed being a scout. More often than not he was on his own, away from the fleet and in deep space, exploring areas that had only been seen by astronomers. According to the regulations, he had given numbers to the stars that weren't in the normal guides, but he was allowed to name any Earth-like planets he discovered. That was why there was a Clark's World and a Randly's Planet, and half a dozen others named after his family or his current girlfriend.

Clark was not a young man by scout standards. He was just over forty and had been flying through space alone for twenty years. At first he had been bothered by the enforced loneliness but quickly grew to enjoy it. There were no commanding officers to harass him about the length of his hair or the fact he hadn't shaved. There were no early morning meetings, no rigid schedules that had to be followed, and no reports to be written until he returned to the fleet. Then, most times, he could find someone who would transcribe his notes for him, or he could use a voice access computer and just talk about his trip.

During the years with the fleet, Clark had been assigned a single ship and had been allowed to modify it. That was one of the rewards for being a scout. Too many couldn't stand the lack of human companions. A deep-space mission drove them to the brink. Clark didn't mind it and the modifications allowed him to take the longest of the missions. He had a library of old Earth movies, books in the computer, and a computer navigation system of his own design that allowed him to sleep twenty hours a day if the mood moved him.

So, when Clark, who had been launched with a dozen other scouts to explore the center of the galaxy, finally located the enemy, he had been asleep. He had been dreaming about a steak dinner, baked potato, and green salad. He'd never eaten a real steak, but had eaten salads and potatoes.

He snapped awake, his attention focused on the radar display in front of him. There was a single target more than five thousand miles from him. He glanced at the navigation console and saw that the closest star system was more than four billion miles away, the star at the center a bright ball of light and off to his right.

"Okay," he said out loud and reached for the joystick. He touched a button so that he had full control of the scout ship. He pushed it to the left and began a rapid turn. He touched the thruster and shot forward, toward the small ship displayed on the radar.

With the forward view screen at full magnification, he could see that the enemy ship, or rather the unknown ship, wasn't much larger than his own. It was a fat orb with stubby wings and a clear canopy set forward. It looked nothing like a fighter or interceptor or even a spacecraft. It looked more like a lifting body designed to fall through atmospheres without incinerating itself. It was not like anything that belonged to any group, race, or planet that he had ever encountered.

"Okay," he said again. He slowed slightly, but kept his nose pointed at the other ship. He activated the computer voice input. "Identify craft located four thousand six hundred miles in front of us."

"No matches found."

"Is the craft manned?"

"Insufficient data."

"Thanks for nothing," said Clark. "Did the craft come from the closest system?"

"Affirmative."

"Number of planets in system?"

"Twenty-two . . . Six inner planets, two in the biosphere. Three that are rocks. Eleven that are gaseous giants on outer edge of the system."

Clark took a deep breath. He rubbed a hand over his face and then turned his attention to the craft. It was closer and seemed to be coming straight at him.

"Okay," he said. He turned to the right and dropped away from the enemy. "Let's see if it follows."

He activated the rear camera and watched the other ship as it blossomed with flame and turned to pursue.

"Okay," he said. "I get it."

Now he accelerated and pulled back on the stick, lifting the nose and beginning a loop. When he was pointed at the enemy ship, he rolled to the right to level out and continued to accelerate. There was no reaction from the other ship.

Clark raced forward, accelerating as he closed the distance. All sensors, radars, and detectors were on. If the enemy didn't know he was there, it would soon see him. He was radiating electromagnetic waves across the spectrum. He'd look like a small star.

"Computer, do you have a reading on any occupants of that craft?"

"Insufficient data."

"Fine. Is that craft armed?"

"Insufficient data."

Clark took a deep breath and kept the nose of his craft pointed at the enemy ship. He didn't waver, holding the stick steady, and continued to accelerate, all instruments searching for additional detail.

"There is a ninety percent probability that the craft contains a single air-breathing occupant."

"Thank you, computer."

Clark decided that he would buzz the enemy ship, photograph it, and then make a run into the planetary system. Then, depending on what he found, he'd head back to the fleet.

"Warning! Warning! Shot detection. Shot detection. Missile has been fired."

Clark jinked right and then left and then fired a flare as he retarded the engine to cut the heat from it. "Type of missile?"

"Radar homing."

"Suppress it."

"Missile launched and homing on intruder," said the computer. "Missile running true. Interception of incoming missile in fifteen seconds . . . Detonation, detonation. Threat has been eliminated."

"Well, now we know," said Clark excitedly. "We'll go after him now."

He pushed the stick forward into a deep dive and continued on around, rolling out heading for the enemy. He accelerated, forcing himself back in his seat. He fired his laser knowing that the beam would be dissipated by the distance. It wouldn't have the power to punch through the enemy ship's skin even if he managed a hit. With the laser firing, he launched two missiles, one behind the other.

The enemy ship dipped and then turned, rolling away from him. The dogfight was taking place at over three thousand miles using sensors and radar. Clark couldn't see the enemy ship visually and knew it couldn't see him.

"Beam weapon," the computer warned. "Outer hull is beginning to heat."

Clark jinked right and then left and the beam slipped off his hull. "Status of missiles," he said.

"Running hot and true. Impact in two minutes fourteen seconds."

Clark had thought about using the enemy's own beam to aim a missile. It could ride the radiation thrown off by the beam for guidance, but that would be wasted if either of his missiles destroyed the target.

"Keep me advised of missile progress."

"Affirmative."

Clark rolled out, pointed his nose at the enemy ship again, and accelerated rapidly. He wanted to close the distance between them and destroy the enemy. At the moment there was too much distance and it gave the enemy pilot too much time to react. A kid with a BB gun could take out the missiles at the distance they were fighting.

"Beam on again. Hull is heating."

Clark jinked up and twisted around, putting a different side of his ship toward the enemy. He began a slow, continuous rotation so that the beam couldn't lock on to a single point to superheat the skin of his ship to punch through it. It was the best defense.

"Two thousand five hundred miles to enemy ship."

Clark checked the heads-up display. The enemy ship was running straight toward him. The closure rate was climbing rapidly.

"Time to impact, one minute thirty seconds. Missiles running true."

Clark watched them as they raced toward the enemy. The heads-up displayed them as pinpoints of light, the track marked in yellow and the enemy ship in flashing red.

"Missile destroyed," said the computer.

There was no spectacular explosion. The first missile blip just disappeared from the HUD. The track faded leaving only the second missile and the enemy ship.

"Second missile destroyed."

Clark hadn't expected either of them to get through. He just wanted the enemy to know that he had some teeth too. He continued to roll, twisting right and left, presenting a difficult target for the enemy. He fired his laser, saw it touch the side of the enemy ship and slide away.

"Distance five hundred miles."

Clark nodded, not realizing that he had. He kept his attention focused on the HUD and the enemy. It was beginning a slow turn as if to retreat into the star system.

"Two hundred fifty miles."

Clark fired the laser, aiming at the tail of the enemy ship. Numbers on the HUD told him that the skin temperature of the enemy ship was increasing rapidly. It spun away, dove straight down, and rolled, breaking the beam lock.

"Fire two more missiles."

"Missiles away. One hundred miles."

The nose of the enemy ship seemed to erupt. Clark knew that it was firing at him, but he ignored it as the distance shrank. They were only fifty miles away from each other. Clark flipped a red cover out of the way and hit the button concealed under it. A spread of torpedoes flashed out. Small weapons that homed on the only heat source around. Clark made sure that the enemy ship radiated heat by keeping the laser beam on it.

"Twenty miles."

Through the tiny windows of the cockpit, Clark actually saw, for the first time, the enemy. The ship was a dark color, barely visible against the backdrop of space, and had they not been close to galactic center, Clark doubted he would have seen it.

"First missile destroyed," announced the computer. "Beam weapon superheating hull."

Clark aimed his ship right at the enemy and kept up the pressure with his laser. The second missile disappeared in a bright flash of light and then the first of the torpedoes struck the enemy ship. There was a flash of light near the nose of the ship, a second one a few feet behind it, and then a brilliant burst of brightness at the center of the enemy craft. An explosion that was hotter than a star flared. Clark turned his head and closed his eyes.

"Enemy ship destroyed," said the computer.

Clark couldn't resist the victory roll. He aimed at the center of the expanding cloud of debris, then pulled up to fly over it and barrel-rolled as he passed it. "Got you, you son of a bitch."

"Enemy craft contained two life forms," the computer announced. "Two escape pods monitored."

"Direction of flight?"

"Toward the star system. Wait one. Target planet is fourth from the star. Intercept possible."

"Life forms on board?"

"Wait one."

Clark turned toward the star system. He couldn't see any of the planets nor could he see the escape pods. They were too small and too far away.

"Probability of life forms in pods is twelve percent," said the computer.

For an instant Clark was confused. Why provide escape pods if not for the crew. Then he thought about the intell probes carried in his ship, that were carried by each of the scout ships. They were designed to home on the fleet rally signal and provide data in the event that his ship was damaged or destroyed and he couldn't report.

"Can we still intercept and destroy?" He was searching for the pods on the heads-up.

"Affirmative."

"Plot course for intercept and destroy each of the pods when possible."

The computer didn't respond. Clark felt the ship turn and accelerate. He leaned back, scanning the instruments and then trying to see something through the tiny windows. A pinpoint of light flared and caught his attention.

"First pod destroyed. Second has entered the star system. Course is unaltered."

"Are any of the planets inhabited?"

"Sensor scans reveal an industrial complex on the fourth planet."

Clark had been a scout long enough to know that the computer hadn't answered the question that he had asked. It told him that there was an industrial complex but that didn't mean the planet contained any life.

"Second pod has been destroyed."

"Decelerate," said Clark.

"Decelerating."

"I have the flight controls again," said Clark.

"Ship control relinquished."

"We will make a quiet pass at the fourth planet and then return to the fleet."

"Orders specify," the computer warned in its flat, mechanical voice, "locate and report all spacefaring entities. The mission has been accomplished."

"I know that," said Clark. He didn't care that he was arguing with a computer. "We will check out that industrial complex first."

CHAPTER
3

Price had decided that he was going to talk to Dr. James in person. A staff meeting with the Colonel sitting in was not the place for him to question the doctor at length. In the doctor's own office, it might be easier to learn more about the alien creature.

Price walked down the corridor where the red lights still burned signaling that the night shift was still working. He stopped outside the morgue. The hatch irised open and bright light spilled out into the corridor. Price entered, surprised to see the staff working so late.

There was an antiseptic cleanliness to the interior. The floors were of polished metal, as were the bulkheads. Clusters of lights were mounted over the autopsy tables. Silver shelves held bottles, flasks, and instruments. White cabinets displayed stainless-steel instruments. Other instruments were placed by the autopsy tables waiting to be used.

One of the women broke away from her work and walked to meet him. She wore a bloodstained white smock and a surgeon's mask. In her right hand she held a knife.

"What can I do for you?"

"What's going on down here?"

"Is that any business of yours?"

Price shook his head. "No, not really. I was looking for Dr. James."

"He's off duty now. What did you want of him?"

Price studied the eyes over the mask. They were bright blue eyes of a shade he'd never seen. She had light blond hair that was as fine as any he'd seen. The slightest motion of her head set it moving.

He fumbled for words and then said, "The autopsy on the alien creature. I wanted to review the notes made on it."

"Mainframe should have it."

"I checked and couldn't find it."

"Then it's classified and if you don't have the codes, then you must not be authorized to see it." She turned.

"Wait," said Price. "Of course I'm authorized. I'm authorized to see everything."

She turned back to face him and pulled down the surgeon's mask. Her mouth was wide and her lips were thin. Hers was not the classic beauty promised by the eyes and the hair and Price wished that she hadn't pulled down the mask. He'd have preferred to let his mind fill in the image.

"Who are you?"

"Price. Military Intelligence. I need access to that material to properly complete my mission."

"Okay, Price, Military Intelligence, come with me and we'll see what we can find."

Price followed her to one of the offices to the side. She turned on the lights and entered, dropping into a chair near the computer. She powered it up, watched the screen, typed in her access code, and finally she typed in a number and rocked back, letting the computer search for the material she wanted.

When the screen brightened, she pushed on the side of the monitor so that Price could see it. "Tell me what you want to see."

"Cause of death if it could be determined."

She put her fingers on the keyboard and typed.

"Nothing," said Price.

She pulled the monitor around and said, "Must be something. Has to be. Damn. That is strange."

"Why wouldn't there be a cause of death listed?"

She looked at him and said, "Could be any one of a number of reasons including that we don't know. It was an alien, after all. Maybe we just couldn't understand why it died."

"What's the file tell you?"

She watched the screen as she scrolled through the data, shaking her head. "This is not complete. Some interesting diagrams . . . hell, this thing didn't have much in the way of a digestive system. The reproductive system doesn't seem to exist. At least I can't see it. Looks like God didn't complete this one before he turned it loose." She looked up at Price. "I didn't do the work on this so I can only guess."

"Is the autopsy complete?"

"Meaning is it ended or was there something left out?"

"I mean, if you had conducted it is there something you would have done that hasn't been?"

She shook her head. "No, doesn't look like it. There are scraps of information missing, but that might be because we're dealing with an alien life form. We don't want to draw conclusions without the proper evidentiary base."

Price took a deep breath. "Then you say there is nothing left out."

"Not that I can see. Is there something specific that you're looking for?"

Price sat back on the corner of the desk and looked at the data on the screen. It meant next to nothing to him yet there was something about the whole thing that bothered him. Unfortunately, he couldn't think of a way to ask the question, or even what the question might be.

"I was just wondering if there was anything irregular about the autopsy."

"Nothing that I can see based on what we have here." She touched a button and let the screen go dark. "Looks to be a very good autopsy."

"Okay," said Price. "I'm surprised, but I bow to your superior knowledge on this."

"Anytime. Anything else you need?"

"What happened to the body? Was it destroyed?"

"Oh, hell no. You don't destroy a unique biological sample. You store it for further research."

Price nodded and then said, "There was another alien species found on the ship . . . all dead. I mean another intelligent species. Anything on that?"

"Not here. That would be over in exobiology. We're only interested in the recent dead. Those bodies that we get to play with."

Price stood up. "Thanks."

"Anytime."

Price left the office and walked to the hatch. When it irised open, he stepped through. The lights in the corridor were now brighter. The new day was beginning. As the hatch shut behind him, Price couldn't help but feel he'd been a victim of a fast shuffle.

When Coollege entered the intell office, Monier was already there with the regimental chief of staff. Major Ralph Reynolds was standing at the console pointing out the controls. There was one document displayed on the center screen, the red top-secret labels flashing brightly.

"Excuse me," said Coollege coolly, "but this is not authorized."

Reynolds completed what he was doing, punched the enter, and then said, "I am providing Lieutenant Monier with a rundown on the operation in here."

Coollege took a deep breath and let it out slowly. "Major, this is a classified operation. The hatch is locked for a reason."

"I am cleared, as is Lieutenant Monier."

"That is not the point. And you may not be cleared for everything that we have in this office or to which we have access. Much of it concerns operations of the ship which is outside your area. You are not supposed to be in here unless one of the people assigned to the office is present."

Reynolds turned around and stared at Coollege. "Lieutenant, I outrank you and I will thank you to remember that."

"Sir, you are in violation of a half-dozen military regulations and security requirements. Not only those of this office but the regiment and the fleet. If you would like to push the matter, I'm sure the provost marshal would be interested in this. You left the hatch unlocked with top-secret material prominently displayed on the main screen and easily visible from the corridor."

Reynolds stood up and it looked as if he was in a rage. His face was red, eyes narrowed, and the veins throbbed in his forehead. And then he laughed. "Of course, Lieutenant. You are absolutely right and I apologize. I should have waited until you were here but the Colonel wanted to have Lieutenant Monier up to speed as quickly as possible."

"Yes, sir."

"If you'll take over."

"Yes, sir."

Reynolds moved to the hatch but stopped before it irised open. "Lieutenant Monier, the Colonel will meet with you for lunch. Please don't be late."

"No, sir."

When Reynolds disappeared, Coollege said, "I'm very sorry about that but the security regulations are very clear on the point."

"You are not sorry," said Monier.

"How would you know?"

"Trust me. I know."

"Just what in the hell are you doing here?" asked Coollege. "You don't seem to have the proper military training. I noticed last night that there are little things . . ."

"I have only been on active duty for a short period. I have some unique talents that were thought to have benefits in intelligence operation."

"Just what do you do?"

Monier sat down and scratched her head. "That is a question that I answer for only a few people . . . but I guess you'd be one of the few."

Price returned to the intell office and found Coollege and Monier sifting through the various records concerning the alien ship and the being on it. He watched them for a moment and then walked forward. To Coollege, he said, "Is she authorized to see all this?"

"Sure, Tree." She picked up a disk and waved it at him. "Complete access to everything we have. Full clearances, confirmed through the ship's office and the regimental headquarters. I could backtrack it to Earth but that would take forever."

Turning to Monier, he said, "I hope you understand the reason for asking."

"Yes, sir."

"Have you spotted anything that we have overlooked?" He took the last available chair.

"No, sir. Not yet."

"Tree," said Coollege, "there is something you should know about Rachel."

"No there isn't," said Price. "I have been briefed by the Colonel. My only question is—"

Monier broke in. "Sorry to interrupt, Captain, but the answer is yes. I really can, though the farther the distance, the more difficult the task. And no, I don't invade privacy. I'm not really sure how to describe it easily. Let me just say you can block me if you want."

Price sat for a moment, trying to think. "I'm trying to think of how to ask this."

Monier said, "I can read the surface thoughts but I can't get much deeper than that. I suppose, if I practiced, I could learn to do it, but I have no desire to penetrate that deeply into the human mind."

"So you can read thoughts."

"To a point. But I think my job here is to . . . see what I can tell from the alien artifacts. To see if I can influence their thinking process by creating random displays for them, and to inhibit their computer functions."

Price shook his head as if to clear it. "Let me have that again?"

"Mental energy," said Monier, "is electrical in nature. As you know, static electricity can cause a computer to introduce random errors. Of course, those are random errors. What we have practiced, on Earth, is to introduce specific errors or to create specific responses on the sensor apparatus. I have practiced this as well and can influence the programming."

She stopped to see if he was still listening and continued, "I have been able to induce specific hallucinations in a cross section of population. Again, I believe it relates to the electrical activity of the brain. And the electrical nature of thought."

She waited to see if he was going to protest her theory. When he didn't, she added, "I can, sometimes, determine facts from holding objects or clothing that belonged to the subject. I think, based on all that, I can determine some facts about the alien objects."

"If true you could be a very valuable asset to this office," said Price. His voice said that he didn't believe it.

"It's true, Captain. I have been reviewing the records of the alien ship for the last several weeks . . . before I arrived here. I'm intrigued by that race you found there. The ones that were all dead, trapped as you were."

"Have you learned anything?"

"No, sir, but then I just got here. If I could handle something from them, I might be able to read them better. I might be able to tell you something."

A thought occurred to Price. "Have you tried to locate the home world of the builders of the asteroid?"

"Yes, sir. We have access to a number of artifacts from it and to all the video and holo of it. I'm afraid that we couldn't get much other than it was from close to the galactic core."

"Hell," said Price, "I could have told you that. This is beginning to sound like the psychics from the past. Could tell you all about your life but couldn't give you the winning lottery numbers or who would win the Superbowl."

"It's not like that," said Monier evenly. "The readings have been unable to provide us with that data at this time. That's one of the reasons I'm here. Maybe if I board the asteroid I can pick up something."

Still skeptical, Price said, "Sure."

"Think of it as one more tool in your arsenal. You don't throw out a rifle because the rifleman misses once in a while. You use it when it fits into the framework of the circumstances."

"Okay," said Price. "I didn't mean to be rude. If you can help us improve our operation, welcome aboard."

"Thank you, Captain."

"Now, is everyone hungry or is it just me. I haven't had any breakfast yet."

"Is that all you people do? Eat? Why don't you all weigh a ton?"

"Because," said Coollege, "we often get sent out to alien planets and we lose all the extra weight we've gained."

"Let's lock up and eat. Then we can get down to work."

"Yes, sir."

CHAPTER

4

Clark wasn't sure how he was going to approach the planet. It was obvious a spacefaring race, proven by the orb that had intercepted him, inhabited the place. The question that had to be answered was if the orb had been a normal picket, out there searching for other spacecraft, or had it been sent up to investigate him specially. Was their detection ability so good that they could spot his tiny ship while it was still in deep space nearly a light-year away?

"Give me a visual on the planetary system," he told the computer.

The computer didn't answer but displayed the system on the HUD, showing the inner planets in red, except for the two in the biosphere that were bright blue, and the outer gas giants in bright green. Pinpricks of light, a dim orange, showed the assorted debris in orbit around all planets.

"Indications of intelligence?"

An arrow appeared pointing to the fourth planet. The computer voice said, "No radiation detected. It is not a radio source."

"Any indications at all?"

"Large-scale structures. Atmosphere is nitrogen oxygen without the abundant traces of carbon dioxide that would be indicative of carbon-based life."

"Has it been abandoned?" asked Clark.

"Insufficient data."

"Flight time to planet?"

"Under current speed, eighteen hours thirty-five minutes. Under masking, twenty-two hours fifteen minutes. Fastest approach could be made in nine hours four minutes."

"Plot quickest and the masked, and display."

"Course is laid in."

Clark studied the data, decided the enemy already knew he was near, and punched in the quickest course. Satisfied with that decision, he said, "Initiate."

Again there wasn't a verbal response. The engines kicked him, pushing Clark back into his seat. Outside the cockpit nothing changed. It was as if he were sitting still, hovering in space.

Then slowly the star began to brighten and it was obvious that the ship was slipping deeper into the system. The gas giants, which had been faint points of light grew into blue-green balls, tiny pinpricks of brightness near them showing the locations of the satellites. One planet had a network of rings that rivaled that of Saturn.

Clark watched one of them slide by. There was no evidence of any type of outpost on it, or on any of them. No lights, no radiation, nothing. Just a big glowing ball of gas orbiting the star.

"Indications of intelligence?" asked Clark again.

"Negative."

That seemed to make no sense, but then, if Earth was abandoned, there would be the cities, filled with machines that would continue to operate, some of them repairing other machines or the buildings. No human life was required now that the machines had been built. At least no humans would be required for a thousand years or more.

"Scan space near us. Any other ships?"

"Scan complete. Nothing sighted."

Clark took a deep breath and rubbed his face. He scratched at his head. It didn't make any sense. It could be that radio was so old-fashioned that they no longer used it. They'd found another way to communicate.

"Continue toward the fourth planet."

The computer said nothing.

They continued on their path, the fourth planet slowly edging around until it was centered on the nose of his ship. There was nothing spectacular about it. The color ran toward a dull reddish-tan. Three moons circled it.

"Signs of a spaceport?"

"Negative. One city located at the north pole. Supporting highways toward the equator but no detectable signs of traffic along them. Underground communication system linked to the major complex at the pole."

"Record all this."

"Recording."

Clark watched the heads-up, looking for anything unusual but found nothing. No craft were launched, no sensors turned toward him, nothing at all.

He kept his attention focused on the planet as it came closer. No lights appeared on the dark side. Nothing to indicate civilization.

The surface changed until he could see continents and oceans, and then lakes and rivers and mountains. No signs of any cities except for the giant one at the top of the world. Not the best place for humans, but then, there was no evidence that humans lived there.

The computer chimed and announced, "Sensors indicate that there are life forms on the planet's surface."

"Location?"

"At the pole."

"Okay," said Clark. "Let's slow down now. Give me a parking orbit twenty thousand miles above the surface. Keep recording all incoming data."

"Acknowledged."

"Give me a magnified view on the heads-up."

"Acknowledged."

Clark studied the image. It was tilted and exaggerated because of the angle and the range. He could detect no movement anywhere on the planet's surface but that didn't surprise him. To see something move, even at full magnification, would have meant that a mountain was adrift.

The tans of the planet's surface gave way to a volcano ring at the southern edges of the giant city. The city itself was a chocolate-brown. Although it was in the twilight zone of the planet, there were no lights.

"We have been swept by strong sensor probes."

Clark nodded but didn't speak.

They slipped into the parking orbit, looking down at the surface of the planet. The city was made up of thousands of concentric rings with roads radiating out from the center like the spokes of a wheel. As they moved out farther, more roads were added so that the distance between the streets remained about the same.

"Sensor sweep again," announced the computer. "Electrical activity increasing."

"I thought you said they didn't use radio," said Clark.

"Affirmative. Identification of shielded wiring carrying heavy electrical impulses. No sign of normal radio communications."

"Great," said Clark. "Have to ask the right questions to get answers around here."

"Sensors have locked on to our craft."

Clark didn't like the sound of that. He glanced out the tiny window but that told him nothing. The data was parading across the HUD. There was no way he could tell if it was a weapons system that locked on, a landing beam designed to assist in descent, or something else. Something that was more menacing.

"Record and then let's break orbit."

"Acknowledged."

Clark continued to study the HUD. Red lights began to appear all over it, showing the locations of potential weapons. The outer ring seemed to bristle with them. The center was nearly all red, suggesting that something there had to be protected—something considered important.

At that moment, as beams began to flash, the ship accelerated, the beams falling away. Some swung toward him, touching the rear of the ship, and then slipped off as he jinked right and left and continued to climb out.

"Missile launched," announced the computer.

"Will it catch me?"

"Insufficient . . . negative. It is falling away."

Clark turned his attention from the HUD to the tiny cockpit windows. He watched as one of the moons slipped past him and noticed a flash of light on the surface of it, near the twilight zone.

"Missile launched," said the computer.

"Evade it."

The ship accelerated suddenly, shoving Clark into his seat. A curtain of black slipped down over his eyes, and he was looking down a long, thin tunnel. Slowly his vision came back.

"Missile evaded. Falling away."

"Sweep the system in front of us. Any indications of enemy ships?"

"Negative."

"Let's just keep accelerating."

Now that they had moved away from the planet and its moons, the sensation of speed was gone again. Clark refused to look out the windows, but watched the distance build as measured by the HUD. He was racing from the enemy system, about to hit light speed.

"Target located directly in front."

"On the heads-up."

It appeared as a tiny flashing light centered on the HUD. The distance to it was just over seven thousand miles. It appeared to be trying to intercept.

"Target type?"

"Insufficient data."

Clark couldn't believe that the object was anything other than another enemy ship. It looked as if it was coming at him. And that, by definition, made it an enemy. Anything coming at him was the enemy until he identified it as friendly. That wouldn't happen here, he was sure of that. He put his hands on the controls.

"Second target located."

"On the heads-up."

As the new target appeared, a third followed quickly and then a fourth. They were spread across the sky, arranged so that one of them would be in a position to intercept him no matter what he did or how he tried to escape. The others would be in a position to back up if he engaged anyone. He could always retreat toward the sun, but if they had been able to get in front of him, there would be a line on the other side of the star ready to intercept.

They could even launch from the planet's surface and still have a good chance of intercepting him.

"How long before I can engage the closest target?"

"At current acceleration, four minutes."

"Course to closest contact. Fire missile as soon as we're at maximum range. I have the controls."

"Acknowledged."

Clark closed his eyes for a moment and took a deep breath. He wiped his hands on his shirt and then gripped the controls. He watched the distance on the HUD shrink. The enemy ship, an orb just like the one he had encountered entering the system, was a small pulsating light on the HUD.

He raced toward the enemy ship, the numbers on the HUD unwinding rapidly. As soon as he was in range with his missiles, the computer locked on the target and fired. Through the tiny window, he could see the pinpoint of light that marked the missile's rocket motor. It faded from sight and he watched the track of the missile and the orb on the heads-up. Thirty seconds later, far short of the target, the missile detonated.

Clark took that as his cue. He shoved the stick forward, dived low, and turned toward the right, away from the path that would take him back to the fleet. He kept an eye on the HUD, watched the enemy ships. The farthest from him took no action, but the three closest turned with him, diving to meet him. He hit a button and dropped a spread of glowing flares.

He accelerated again, pushing for light speed. He kept his attention focused on space in front of him. Safety was there, if he could break out of the system.

"Missile fired."

"Rear view on the HUD."

Only two of the enemy ships showed, both aimed right at him. The missile was a tiny point with a yellow tail. It didn't seem to be closing the distance.

"How soon to light speed?"

"Transition in two minutes."

Clark grinned. He was going to win again. He kept the stick shoved forward, watching the enemy ships as they fell farther astern. The missile trail flashed and faded as the weapon stopped accelerating when its fuel was exhausted. Evading it was no longer a problem. But the closest of the enemy ships fired a spread of missiles. Four of them designed to prevent him from turning back on them for the moment. Clark wasn't worried by the tactic.

"Give me a spread of mines across our trail."

"Mines dispersed. Transition to light in one minute thirty seconds."

But Clark wasn't interested in that. He was watching the enemy orbs as they shot forward, at the string of mines that he'd laid. The lead ship passed close to one and it detonated, the fireball growing brightly to engulf the enemy. A secondary explosion flared and faded. The enemy was gone, now only a growing cloud of debris.

"Transition to light in one minute."

The remaining two enemy ships kept coming. One fired another missile but it malfunctioned, spinning off to the left and detonating suddenly. The second enemy ship seemed to decelerate and began to fall away. It could no longer keep up with the chase through the system.

"Their equipment sucks," laughed Clark.

"Ten seconds to light speed."

Clark braced himself, felt a slight shudder in the ship, and everything outside shifted suddenly, blurring to the red. As he crossed over, he began a long, looping turn back toward the fleet. The HUD was clear, the enemy ships having been left behind him.

"Distance to system end," said Clark.

"One minute. Distance to the fleet now four days."

"Let's just keep accelerating."

CHAPTER 5

Price held the plastic envelope out and said, "I almost had to sign my life away to get this. It has been put through the decontamination process. No evidence of any biological contamination. It's safe to handle."

Monier took the bag from him but didn't open it. She held it up to the light and examined it. "This came from the uniforms of the aliens?"

"Those we found inside the ship. They didn't build it. I think they were trapped like us. You think you'll be able to read anything from it?"

She dropped to the console and studied it. "I should be able to pick up something." She leaned forward, her elbows on either side of the plastic bag.

"We have drawn some conclusions based on what we saw while on the ship."

"I don't want to know it," said Monier. "Not at the moment. I don't want to be influenced."

"Okay," said Price.

Monier pushed the bag with a finger and then opened it, but didn't reach in. She pushed it around carefully, gingerly, as if she expected it to suddenly come alive. "I can't tell much about it."

Price didn't respond.

Finally she picked up the bottom of the bag and shook the patch out of it. It dropped on the console. She touched it with a fingernail and then sat bolt upright. Her eyes glazed over and she threw her head back.

"Fear!" She shouted the word and then fell silent.

"What's happening?" asked Price.

"Quiet," she hissed. She now held the patch clasped in both hands. Her eyes were closed and her head tilted back. "There is something in there with them . . . something that followed them from the surface of their planet."

"That explains where it came from," said Price but this time Monier didn't respond to him.

"We can't get out," she said almost hysterically. "We can't get out! Help me!"

Price stood up and moved away from her, watching her. Her face had turned bright red and she was tugging at the collar of her uniform with a finger hooked just inside it.

"We're running out of air. Can't breathe."

That had been what Price had thought when he'd found the bodies on the alien asteroid. They had all suffocated. It was obvious that they had died never realizing there was a breathable atmosphere on the asteroid, but that was not what he wanted to know. He wanted to learn what he could about the race that had been trapped inside it. Where'd they come from. The level of their civilization. . . . The very details of their personal lives, the way they interacted could be left to the exo-anthropologists and sociologists and others. Military intelligence was what he was after.

At first, Price wasn't sure how to react to Monier's display. Then he realized that Monier was not under hypnosis or in a drug-induced trance. He could ask his questions without fear of breaking her concentration or disrupting her train of thought.

"How'd they get to the asteroid?"

"Came into our system. Astronomers spotted it. Tracked it as it neared our home. It came into orbit around our planet. Missiles fired at it disappeared . . ."

"Do you have interstellar flight?" asked Price, not realizing that he had slipped into interrogating Monier as if she were one of the aliens.

"We can travel inside our system. To our moons and the closest of the planets. We do not leave our system. Faster-than-light travel is not possible and the distances are so vast."

Questions blossomed in his mind. Hundreds of them. History questions. Military questions. Life-style questions. Suddenly he was caught up in the situation. He had a conduit into a new civilization.

"We're going to die," she wailed. "There is nothing we can do but sit here and die." She fell silent and then said, "At least the tramoi will die with us."

"Tramoi?" asked Price.

"A predator . . ."

She went on to describe it, but Price was no longer interested in it. He had seen the tramoi and had helped kill it. It was nothing more than an animal . . . with a cunning and slyness that made it dangerous, but it didn't have rational thought. It wasn't an intelligent, tool-building creature.

He didn't want his attention diverted. There were things that he had to find out and most important among those things was to learn how long ago they reached the asteroid. A race that didn't have spaceflight a hundred years ago might have developed it by now. That was the critical question.

"How long ago did the asteroid penetrate your system?"

She said something that made no sense to Price. And then he realized that she was saying that the asteroid had been traveling at under the speed of light. A general survey of the surrounding star systems, as had been launched by the Colonel, should locate that race quickly, though there was no reason for speed. They were stuck in their own system and posed no threat to the fleet or to the Earth.

"There is blackness," she said, interrupting his train of thought.

Price was momentarily confused and then asked, "You're getting all that from the patch?"

Monier ignored the question. "I'm not scared anymore. The tramoi won't be able to kill me. I'll be dead in a short time."

Monier shook herself and opened her eyes. She looked around like she had just awakened. Sweat was beaded on her forehead and stained her uniform. Her hair was plastered to her head. She looked as if she had just stepped from the shower. She slumped back into the chair and took a deep breath. She wiped the sweat from her face.

"I didn't expect that. Death always impresses the images so vividly."

"Any idea how long they have been dead?"

Monier shook her head, her breathing still ragged, as if she'd run a long distance. "Awhile. No way to tell. Images fade with time and these were very crisp, but that doesn't really mean much."

"We have to put together a report for the Colonel about these . . . beings."

"They're no threat to us," said Monier. "They fear that creature, that tramoi, but have the power to wipe it from the face of their planet. They don't because they believe that everything has its role in the universe and to destroy a creature because it is dangerous or because they fear it is a crime against . . ." She stopped talking for a moment and then said, "I guess the best word would be God."

"Interesting," said Price.

"I'll need to give some of this to the anthropologists," said Monier.

"First we let the Colonel have a look. Prepare a classified report for him."

"Of course."

"The danger lies in the direction of the builders of the asteroid," said Price.

"I think so."

Price fell back in his chair, then laughed. "This is a hell of a way to gather intelligence. I'm not sure of how much of it I accept."

Monier took offense. "You will find that about ninety percent of the information I gave you is accurate. As accurate as it can be considering I have to deal with an alien mind to get it. This technique has been well documented by scientists on Earth. This is a legitimate method of gathering data."

"It still seems fanciful to me," said Price.

"But you're going to report to the Colonel."

"Of course. I'm not going to reject a source of information because I find it a little unusual. We'll forward it just as soon as we finish it."

"Yes, sir."

Price, stripped to the waist, with a towel around his neck, sat on his cot in his tiny cabin and wondered just what the hell was next. First he was captured by an alien spacecraft, and managed to escape. Then he's presented with an officer whose claim to fame seemed to be psychic ability. An ability apparently endorsed by higher headquarters. If the brass hadn't believed the skill was real or that the information would be accurate, Monier would still be on Earth. Her orders attested to the faith placed in her by the officers at headquarters.

There was a quiet chime and Price glanced at the hatch. He stood up and touched a button so that the hatch irised open. "Come on in."

Coollege did as told and said, "I can come back later if you're busy."

Price rubbed the towel over his head, almost as if his hair were wet. He tossed the towel to his cot and asked, "What can I do for you?"

"What's the real story on this Monier?"

"I thought we had covered that."

"There are rumors floating around the ship. There are a lot of very worried people."

Price grabbed a shirt and put it on but didn't bother to button it. "What are they worried about?"

Coollege turned her back and stared down into the tiny sink as if there were something fascinating trapped in it. Without looking at Price, she said, "It's that mind-reading thing. I think I understand it. Hell, Tree, we all have secrets, fantasies, things we've done that we're afraid others will learn. People are afraid that all their dirty little secrets will be exposed."

Grinning broadly, Price said, "What could you possibly have hidden in your past that you don't want anyone to know, Jackknife?"

"It's all relative, isn't it. Things that might not embarrass you could embarrass me."

"I spent most of the day with her and she didn't read my mind."

"How do you know?"

Price sat down on his cot and thought about it. "I don't know. But then, she explained all this to us."

"And you believe it?"

"For the moment, yes. But even if she can read deeply, there isn't anything that I can do about it. She's assigned to our shop and I don't have the authority to get rid of her unless she violates security."

"Tree, this really scares me."

Price studied her. "Why?"

"I've tried to explain it. Hell, do you want someone looking into your brain. The Colonel says something stupid and you know it's stupid but do you want that thought available to others. Or maybe you don't like someone because of his color. You want that out—that you have a racist bend to your nature. Or that you don't like working with women because you think they get their positions with their bodies. Or . . ."

"I get the picture," he said, holding up his hand to stop her. "I still don't see the problem."

"I don't want someone around who has that ability."

Price hung his head and stared at the deck under his feet. He'd just watched Monier come up with a picture of life on another planet based solely on her impressions from a scrap of cloth. What he didn't know was if that picture was accurate. If it was, that meant her ability was real. If not, it meant the whole thing was a parlor trick that had no relevance to his operation or to his life.

"We don't know that she can read minds," said Price.

"But if she can?"

"I don't know," he said. "You're basing everything on speculation."

"So you're going to let it go."

"Let's just say that I'm going to wait and see. There's nothing else to do."

Coollege stood there silently and then said, "We going to get something to eat?"

Price rubbed his neck and looked up at her. "You sure you want to eat?"

"At the moment, yes. I want to eat."

"Okay, we can go eat." Price buttoned his shirt and tucked it in. He glanced around the cabin to make sure that everything was secure and that he was leaving nothing out that had to be put away. Satisfied, he said, "Let's go."

The dining facility, which had once been called a mess hall, would have rivaled a fancy restaurant on Earth. It was filled with tables with sparkling white cloths on them. Red napkins were standing on each plate of fine china. The silverware was gleaming and the glasses were crystal-clear. Two of the bulkheads had been paneled with dark wood from the rain forests on Earth. Another of the bulkheads was a real-time holo of space outside the ship. Drifting in formation around them was the rest of the fleet.

Price found a table and sat down. He took the folded napkin, shook it out, and placed it in his lap. When Coollege was settled, he said, "You really want to eat."

"Now that we're here, why not?"

Price turned and watched the shifting of the fleet as it moved. The backdrop of stars, some of them brilliant white, others orange and yellow and red, didn't seem to be moving at all. Had the fleet been ocean-going vessels, it would have seemed they were at anchor. In space, with the distances so vast, it seemed they weren't moving at all.

Coollege followed his gaze and asked, "Why are we at sublight speed."

"Searching," said Price. "Scouts are out, searching for the enemy. No reason to burn up fuel in faster-than-light without knowing where we're going."

"Galactic center," said Coollege.

"That's a huge target. Better to poke along at sublight than waste the fuel."

Coollege took her napkin and examined it. "Sometimes," she said, "I just don't understand what in the hell is going on. We could have bare tables, paper napkins, and metal dishes . . ."

"Morale," said Price. "Gives everyone a feeling of importance. And besides, paper napkins are wasteful but cloth ones can be recycled endlessly. Makes more sense than a paper stock that would either have to be dumped into space or stored on board to be recycled later."

"They think of everything," said Coollege.

"You can bet there is some bean counter sitting on the Colonel's staff who makes sure that we are operating on the lowest possible budget. Certainly don't want to waste a nickel."

"The taxpayers are probably happy with that attitude."

Price looked at her and asked, "You really want to get into this?"

"Meaning?"

"Well, things have been sailing along smoothly but you've just opened a can of political worms. There are times when the bean counters, insisting on the cheapest course, end up causing us to waste a lot of money."

"No, Tree, I don't want to get into this. I'd like to know just one example of the bean counters opting for the cheapest and then costing money."

"Replacement parts," said Price. "You buy the cheapest machine and the contractor, knowing that he is going to lose money on the deal, also knows that he can make it back with spare and replacement parts."

"I hadn't thought of that."

Price grinned broadly. "Sometimes, late at night, in my cabin, I think about that . . . and that this ship was built by the lowest bidder. If we blow up in space, who's going to know the reason why. We just blew up."

"Thank you for that lovely thought," said Coollege. "I know that I'll sleep better tonight."

A shadow fell across the table and when they looked up, Monier said, "I thought I'd find you here."

Coollege looked disgusted. She kept her eyes focused on the table.

Monier asked, "Why are you angry?"

"You knew we'd be here. Knew it. Not thought it. And if you can't read minds, how'd you know what I was thinking?"

"I don't know what you're thinking," said Monier. "I could see that you were angry. Your body language shouted it to me. You don't have to be psychic to see it."

Price laughed and waved a hand. "Join us. Jackknife will get over her mad quick enough."

"No, Captain, thank you. I think that I'll go back to my quarters." She turned and walked stiffly from the dining hall.

"Nicely done, Jackknife. There was no reason for that," said Price.

"Maybe not, but at least we get to eat our dinner alone."

"Right."

CHAPTER 6

He had outrun their chase ships, dodged them and outfoxed them as he had jinked and danced through their star system. He'd left them far behind him, wondering exactly what he was going to do next and what his destination could be.

As soon as he was sure that they weren't in pursuit, he began a long looping turn and headed for the fleet. He'd found the answer to the question. He'd found a spacefaring race that guarded its system with firepower, and even if it wasn't the one for which they searched, it was a hostile one. It was the enemy.

Once he knew he was clear, Clark sank back in the seat, lowered the back so that he was nearly stretched out flat, and then scanned the HUD. Nothing of importance showed anywhere near him.

He reached out and touched a button. The HUD disappeared, replaced by a holographic display warning him that duplication of the copyrighted material was punishable by a stiff fine and more than a year in prison. He wondered how they would find out that he had made an unauthorized copy of the holo and then how they would prosecute him if they did. And a year in prison didn't frighten him.

He dimmed the cockpit lights, engaged the computerized auto-

matic pilot with the course to the fleet plotted, and sat back to
watch. The warning faded into a six-inch-high woman dancing
slowly. She was joined by a man and together they disappeared.
The story was about to begin.

It was a silly story of a man about to be launched into space
and who wouldn't return for more than two years. A story of sepa-
ration and how the man and the woman lived with that problem.
And while he thought it silly, there was nudity in it, and that was
one of the criteria he used to judge a holo. As long as he got
to see some flesh, the story didn't mean much.

But the story was *so* silly that he couldn't stay awake. He fell
asleep and didn't awaken until the computer chimed. He noticed
the holo was replaced by the HUD.

"Target approaching."

"Identity?"

"Rock and metal. Sensors indicate it to be natural."

"You woke me to tell me that . . . avoid it."

"Action initiated. Target to the starboard. Range is two thousand meters."

Clark looked out the window and thought that he could see
the asteroid but wasn't sure. It was too dark.

"I assume that there is no one aboard that rock."

"Negative biological indications."

Clark straightened up and raised the back of his seat. He
scrubbed his face roughly with both hands and then stretched as
much as he could in the confined area of the cockpit. "Distance
to fleet?"

"Twenty-seven hours at current speed."

"Let's punch it up," said Clark. "I want to get there as quickly
as possible."

"Acknowledged."

Clark scanned the HUD and found it clear. He lowered the
rear of his seat again and said, "I don't want to be awakened
for natural phenomenon. Evade it and return to course. I want
to be at the fleet as quickly as possible."

"Acknowledged."

Clark leaned back and then closed his eyes. There was no
sensation of motion, just the quiet sounds of the craft in space.
The hum of the computer circuits, the pinging of the sensors as

they searched for the enemy or anything that might be in his way, and the groaning of servos as they kept the ship on the proper course.

Normally he couldn't hear the sounds or ignored them. At the moment they were comforting, letting him know that the ship was functioning properly. They relaxed him just as the ticking of a clock sometimes relaxed small animals.

When he awakened, the HUD showed nothing new. He was still in deep space away from planetary systems and artificial ships. He scanned the other instruments and found nothing of interest there.

"Distance to the fleet?"

"One hour."

"Show me on the HUD."

A series of flashing yellow lights appeared. The distance in miles was shown, as well as the flying time. Clark rubbed his hands together, moved his seatback to the full upright position, and said, "I have the controls."

"Acknowledged."

"Activate the IFF so that they know who we are."

"Acknowledged."

Clark settled in to watch as the numbers on the HUD wound down as the distance to the fleet slipped away. He kept his hand on the control stick though there was no reason for it. There was nothing for him to hit. But sitting in the cockpit, controlling the ship, made him feel as if he were doing something important and that helped keep him awake.

"Time to decelerate from light," announced the computer.

"I know," snapped Clark. He pulled back on the throttle but there was no immediate change. Then the stars seemed to come into focus and Clark was sure that he felt a shifting in his stomach as he slipped through the transition from light speed to sublight.

"Give me a view of the fleet."

On the HUD the first of the ships appeared. It was a distant speck barely visible against the backdrop of space. He punched it up and got his first good look at the fleet. The flagship was hidden in the middle of the formation. It was no larger than any of the others. There was nothing to distinguish it from the rest of the fleet. Nothing that would cause an enemy to notice it.

"Begin the landing sequence," said Clark.

"Acknowledged."

His computer was now communicating with the computer in the landing bay of the flagship. All he had to do was obey the instructions on the HUD for landing. It was almost like the computer simulations used to teach the technique.

He wound his way among the ships of the fleet and aimed at the center of the flagship. As he neared it, approaching slowly, a large hatch near the rear began to open. Bright lights around flared and began flashing. The interior, now visible, had a bright yellow line of lights down the center. Against the far bulkhead were red and green lights.

Clark centered his ship using the lights and then leaned back, letting the computer handle the problem of landing. He just didn't feel like doing it himself.

He slipped over the threshold and was inside the flagship. The hatch irised closed and bright lights burst on. The glass of the windows darkened so that the light didn't momentarily blind Clark.

There was a slight bump as his ship contacted the deck, and then the computer shut down the various systems, keeping the life support on for the moment. Clark unbuckled his restraints, reached out, and patted the instrument panel. "Nice job," he said.

"Thank you," said the computer, the voice suddenly deep and husky.

Clark pushed himself from the seat, cracked the hatch, and saw a contingent coming across the hangar deck toward him. "Well, I guess it's time to go to work."

Price was wedged against the bulkhead in his cot, his arm on fire because he couldn't move it without waking Coollege. Finally, he could take it no longer and he tried to slip it free, but she rolled toward him and opened her eyes.

"You awake?" she asked.

"You know that we shouldn't be doing this," said Price. "Upsets the chain of command. Underminds my authority. All rules, regulations, and common sense say that we shouldn't be doing this."

Grinning, she asked, "Are you afraid that I won't respect you in the morning?"

"No," said Price, laughing. "It's just, well, you know as well as I. You've had the officer's training."

"This is different," said Coollege. "Our relationship isn't just commander and subordinate . . ."

"You trying to convince me or yourself?" interrupted Price.

"Probably a little of both."

There was a quiet chime at the hatch. Price glanced at it and said, "I've got to get up. Probably the Colonel wanting to know what the hell we think we're doing."

"I know what we're doing."

Price lifted himself up and crawled over the top of Coollege, tugging at the sheet so that he could look down at her naked body. She jerked the sheet from his fingers and covered herself.

Price touched a button on the keyboard of his computer so that the screen brightened, showing him who stood in the corridor.

"What can I do for you?"

"Captain Price? Colonel wants a debriefing held now. In the main conference room."

"Right now?"

"Yes, sir."

"I'll be there in ten minutes."

"Yes, sir. Thank you, sir. By the way, do you know where I can find Lieutenant Coollege? She's not in her quarters."

"I'll alert her."

"Thank you, sir."

As soon as the screen darkened, Coollege asked, "What in the hell is this all about?"

"I don't know for sure. Just that we need to get over to the conference room. Maybe one of the scouts has returned."

Coollege threw off the sheet and stood up. She searched the deck near her feet but couldn't find any of her clothes. "I'm going to need to get to my cabin for a clean uniform."

Price found his pants and picked them up. "You'd better hurry. We don't want to have to explain why it took so long to find you."

"Thanks for the help."

He grabbed a shirt and draped it over his shoulders like it were a cape. "You'd better hurry," he advised again.

Coollege had put on her pants without worrying about her underwear. "If you come by to get me, then we can enter together and no one will wonder about it."

"I'm not sure that will work but you go ahead and I'll swing by your cabin."

She struggled into her shirt. She slipped her shoes on her bare feet. "I'll get the rest of my stuff later."

Price sat on the bed and pulled on his socks. "As soon as I'm done, I'll get over to your cabin."

Coollege ducked her head and opened the hatch. She disappeared through it. As she did, Price said to himself, "I can't believe this. First time and the Colonel wants us."

At the hatch outside the conference room, Coollege leaned close and said, "You don't suppose the Colonel knows, do you?"

"We'll find out in a minute. Depends on what happened inside."

The hatch irised open and Price stepped through. The Colonel, looking as if he'd just come from the parade ground, sat at the head of the long, highly polished table. Several staff officers were scattered around in various uniforms and in various states of consciousness. One man had laid his head on the table and was snoring.

"Come in," said the Colonel. "Grab a seat. Do you know Randly Clark? Scout pilot?"

Price nodded. "Sure. We've worked together on a number of projects. Clark?" Price held a hand out across the table.

Clark, his bloodshot eyes ringed in black making it look as if he hadn't slept in a week, half stood. Despite all the sleep he'd just had, he looked tired. He touched Price's hand and dropped back into his seat. "Captain."

The Colonel turned his attention to another on the staff and asked, "Has the computer data been downloaded?"

"Yes, sir. Use Scout One as the access code."

The Colonel pulled his keyboard around, typed quickly, and then sat back. The area above the center of the table began to cloud up, the colors swirling about a foot above the surface. It shimmered and seemed to solidify, finally becoming a picture of a planetary system as seen from deep space. Tiny points of light marked the location of other ships.

Clark said, "I ran into what I would call picket ships outside their system. They attacked me, firing first. I fought back, destroying a couple of them."

"They fired first," said the Colonel.

"Yes, sir. Computer logs will confirm."

The computer expert interjected, "Computer confirms. There was no evidence of tampering."

"Thank you," said the Colonel.

Clark stood up and pointed into the holographic projection. "It seems that they came from this system. They were scattered around the perimeter of it. I engaged one in my path, that attacked me, and then entered the system. One planet appeared to be inhabited. Or rather showed signs of industrial development."

The scene changed showing them the entire planet with all its oceans, continents, mountain ranges, rivers, and lakes marked. There seemed to be no cities, other than a single megastructure sitting on the north pole. The empty land, that which might have been forested or used in agricultural production, gradually gave way to that which looked like desert sprinkled with lava beds that finally became the outskirts of the city.

"Computer, sensors, radars, found no evidence of life on that planet," said Clark. "But then, something was there because I was fired on by missiles."

The holographic model continued to rotate slowly so that each of the people around the table got a good look at everything. Clark narrated his adventure, explaining everything that had happened to him, what his impressions were, where the enemy had been concentrated, and what tactics he had employed.

When that ended and the planet was again hovering above the table, the Colonel asked, "Are there any questions?"

Price said, "I take it that you were unable to detect signs of life."

"That was the one thing that bothered me," said Clark. "It seems to me that we have a new city . . . that it has been repaired and kept up. I mean, it didn't give the appearance of being abandoned. But there were none of the telltale signs of life. I couldn't tell enough about the landscape to determine if there were cultivated areas. Maybe that can be determined."

The computer expert said, "We are looking into it but at the moment I don't have an answer."

Now the Colonel looked directly at Price. "Can we make the assumption that the planet Clark found is the one that built the asteroid?"

"Not at this moment," said Price. "We just don't have enough to go on. If we . . . if Clark could have gotten us a prisoner or some close-up pictures . . ." He held up a hand to stop Clark from protesting. "I know the problems and I don't mean this as a criticism. I'm merely saying that without more data we can't form an opinion. I don't know."

"I think that is something we need to determine," said the Colonel.

"If I might, Colonel," said Clark. "We do have some data. These people in their pickets didn't even try to make contact. They attacked. Period. We have a hostile race that can put ships into space and I think that is something that needs to be explored."

"But you saw nothing there, the sensors picked up nothing that indicated there was anything living on the planet?" asked the Colonel.

Price said, "We didn't have any indication that there was anything living on the asteroid."

"That was because the single individual had been in a state of hibernation. That could explain why we didn't detect the fact."

"You can't be suggesting that the entire population of the planet is hibernating."

"We don't have the data to know anything," said Coollege. "We have more to learn."

The Colonel turned to his chief of staff. "Davis, we have anything from the other scouts?"

"No, Colonel. Latest reports are negative. They have found nothing."

"Okay, then what I want us to do is plan for a mission into that planetary system. Fleet course will be altered so that we are heading in that direction. We will, of course, require more intelligence. Price, you can have what you need. Any questions?"

"Colonel, you can't be saying that we're going to invade this planet based on an assumption of hostility from a single scout."

"I'm saying that we will prepare if the facts warrant it. At the moment it does no harm to begin the preparations. If the intelligence suggests something else, then we can cancel the plan."

"Yes, sir."

"Anything else?"

Price said, "I'd like access to all data about the being from the asteroid. I've been blocked from some of it."

"There are good reasons for wanting it?"

"If this is the enemy, I'm going to have to know as much about it as I can," said Price. "Otherwise my briefings will be incomplete."

"Get with me in the morning." The Colonel touched his keypad and the planet vanished. "I know that I don't have to warn any of you to keep this quiet for a moment. Let's get to work." With that he headed to the door.

As the Colonel left, Coollege leaned close to Price. "There a real reason you want access to the autopsy material?"

"Yeah," said Price. "There is something going on here that I don't like and I want to make sure that I have the answers before we get to the enemy's planetary system."

"You think that Clark found the wrong place?"

"I don't think anything at the moment. I just have some questions that haven't been answered."

"So what are you going to do?" asked Coollege.

"At the moment, I think that I'll go back to bed. Let the computers have some time with the data and then take a look at it in the morning."

"And what do you think I should do?"

Price couldn't help himself. He laughed and said, "Why, I think you should go to bed too."

"I was hoping you'd say that."

CHAPTER
7

Monier sat in the intelligence office, in front of the main viewer, the computer record from the scout ship playing in front of her. She watched the images as they paraded across the screen, aware of other images marching through her mind. Fleeting images that were more shadow than substance.

When the hatch behind her chimed softly before opening, she hit the cut-off button and the image on the screen faded, but not those in her mind. She saw a group of humanoid creatures that had a feline look, with hair on the forearms and the legs below the knees but almost none on the head. She didn't understand the vision but was sure that the beings were not native to the planet.

The hatch irised open and both Price and Coollege entered. Monier glanced over her shoulder at them, looked back at the blank screen, and then suddenly at the two others. "So that is the way it is."

Coollege stopped in her tracks. "Is there anyone on this ship who minds his own business?" Then she remembered who Monier was and what the rumors said. She felt her face grow hot and knew that she was turning red. To hide it, she moved quickly to the console and bent over it as if to study it carefully.

Then she whirled, stared at Monier, and flared. "You just stay the hell away from me."

"I didn't do anything," said Monier.

"Keep your comments to yourself. I don't want you playing with my mind. You hear me?"

Monier looked at Price helplessly and then said, "I didn't read your mind. I didn't read anyone's mind. I don't read anyone's mind without their permission."

"Bullshit," snapped Coollege. "No wonder no one trusts you with you slinging the bullshit like that."

Again Monier looked at Price. She didn't say anything in response.

Price shrugged at her and said, "Let it go, Jackknife."

"Why should I? She's the one causing the trouble." Coollege turned to face him, her fists on her hips, her eyes unblinking.

"This is completely irrational," said Price. "Lieutenant Monier is an officer and by definition she is trustworthy. If you have evidence to the contrary . . ."

"Just having her here," said Coollege.

"Okay," said Price, his voice hardening. "That was the put up or shut up, Lieutenant. Now, if you have no evidence that Monier has been anything but honorable, I will thank you to shut the fuck up. If she has behaved in a way that is not prescribed by regulations, you present your evidence. If not, then shut up. I am tired of this now. Lieutenant Monier will be given the benefit of the doubt. Do I make myself clear?"

Coollege stood stiffly, staring at Price, and then lowered her eyes. "I understand, Captain."

"You two don't have to be friends, but you will work together. Neither of you has a choice in this matter. Is that understood?"

Coollege nodded and Monier said, "Yes, sir."

"Good," said Price. He let things settle for a moment and then asked Monier, "What have you been doing this morning?"

"Reviewing the material brought in last night. I'm afraid that I haven't come up with anything extraordinary though."

Price sat down and twisted around in the chair. He leaned both elbows on the desk and said, "Tell me what you have."

"Just a few impressions. I understand, from the computer file, that the scout didn't find any sign of a biological race on the planet."

"He found evidence that someone had been there once but nothing current."

"I get the impression that they were still there."

"Our instruments would have picked them up if they were there in any concentration."

Monier shrugged. "I don't want to argue the value of the instruments but it is possible that the enemy has developed some kind of a masking device."

"To what purpose?" asked Coollege.

"That I don't know but I can speculate. They have sent out one probe . . ."

"Yeah," interrupted Price. "One that we know about. I would assume they sent others throughout the galaxy. That's not the sort of thing you do only once."

"So," said Monier, "they have the ability to do it and they know the capabilities of their device. Now, suppose they assume there are other races with a technology equal to theirs. In other words, they take steps to hide their existence from anyone who comes looking."

"You base that on anything other than speculation?"

"That and the fact that I believe there are people on that planet but our instruments couldn't find them."

"Jackknife, why don't you lock the door. Let's review what the scout has and see if there is anything there that was overlooked."

"Sure," said Coollege.

For the next hour they watched the main screen as the images flashed. They focused on small sections and magnified them as much as possible. They found separate buildings, they saw some plant life, trees, bushes, and even flowers growing at the sides of some of the buildings. They spotted what looked to be railroad tracks that hadn't been used for a long time. Gaps in the roadbed and the reddish color of the rails suggested that, though Price wasn't sure that engineers on another planet would build a railroad using iron rails.

But for all the searching they could find no evidence of any movement or any means of transportation other than the tracks.

No rolling stock was visible. No cars or trucks on the roads and certainly nothing in the air.

Price rocked back in his chair, laced his fingers behind his head, and said, "You think that the pickets radioed a warning and everyone took cover?"

"That'd never work on Earth," said Coollege. "There would always be someone who didn't get the word. Even the fastest survey conducted by the enemy would catch some people in the street."

"I'd have to agree," said Monier. "Hell, you'd have some people trying to be clever spelling out words to greet the visitors."

"If a state of war existed?" said Price.

"Even then," said Coollege. "There is always someone who has the dissenting view or believes the enemy is right and we are wrong. You just couldn't do it."

"So, if they did," said Price, "that tells us something more about them. Just as sticking one of their people on a ship that stayed in space for fifteen thousand years told us something."

Price stood up and walked around his chair. He glanced back up at the screen and then walked to it, staring up at it. "Let's get some of this into the computer for the Colonel. We'll have to label it speculation, but then, that's what we're supposed to do. Speculate . . . no analysis," Price corrected himself. "This is analysis."

"I'd like some more information to work with," said Coollege.

"They'll probably send in more scouts now that they've scored a hit," said Price. "They'll need to gather more information as quickly as they can."

"And warn the enemy."

"Wait a minute," said Price. "We're assuming that we have an enemy. They might be the most friendly people in the world . . . make that galaxy."

"Except that they fired on the scout the first chance they got," Coollege reminded him.

Clark found that he couldn't get comfortable on the ship. He had too much space. He had a private cabin and if that had seemed cramped, which it didn't, he could have walked out into the corridor that, to him, seemed to go on forever.

He sat on the cot and stared at the deck, hugging himself and wishing that he could get off the ship. That was the thing about him. The older he got, the less he liked having to be on the main ships. They were too big and had too many people on them. If he could just dock with them for supplies and fuel, dispose of the waste on his ship, and replenish his supply of holographic movies, he would be happy.

He heard the quiet chime near the hatch and for a moment didn't know what it meant. He remembered and touched a button letting the hatch iris open.

Price stood there and asked, "Mind if I come in?"

"I'm very tired," said Clark.

"I can imagine. But I have a couple of questions that I wanted to ask outside the normal channels. Nothing on the record. Just your impressions, right or wrong."

Clark stepped back to allow Price to enter. He didn't like being that close to another human. He felt his space was being invaded. He was nervous, wanting to retreat as far from Price as he could.

"Mind if I sit down?" asked Price.

Clark pointed at the chair. "Go ahead."

Price sat down and studied the scout for a moment. "You get any feeling about the opposition?"

"Meaning?"

"You said that they fired on you the instant they spotted you."

"And got into range. Or what they thought of as being in range."

"What did you think about that?"

Clark closed his eyes, as if putting himself back into that time and then shook his head. "Nothing. I was mainly interested in evading their missiles. I didn't think about it one way or another."

Price rubbed the back of his neck. "I'm not sure exactly what I'm looking for here. You didn't get a chance to see any of your adversaries, did you?"

"What do you expect? That they made some kind of radio or video contact?"

"It's a thought," said Price.

"I have no idea what they looked like. I have provided pictures of their ships, their home world and city, and the system where I found it. I provided everything that I was required to supply."

"Yeah," said Price. "But you have no clue."

"No, Captain. I have no clue. I saw absolutely nothing other than their ships and their world. Hell, for all I know, those ships could have been controlled robotically."

"You think of anything else," said Price, "you let me know. I've got to have some answers but I don't have any."

"I might be going out on a mission soon," said Clark. "Very soon."

"If you do, please stop by the intell office before you go, just in case I've thought of something else."

Clark moved to the hatch and stood there as it irised open. When Price didn't stand, he said, "I'm very tired, Captain." He gestured toward the open hatch.

"Sure." Price stepped to the hatch, hesitated, and then left.

When Price was gone, Clark sat down on his cot again. Finally he stretched out and rolled to his side so that he was staring at the bulkhead. He jammed his knees up against it, almost as if bracing himself in his cot, and in seconds was asleep.

Price was walking down the dimly lighted corridor, wondering why they were running on red when it was the middle of the day, when he heard a voice behind him. He turned and saw Sergeant Wallace Stone hurrying toward him.

"Captain, we've been alerted."

"Alerted for what?"

"Recon mission. The Colonel isn't completely happy with the intelligence that has been gathered by his scouts to this point. He wants more data before he can make a command decision."

"Shit," said Price. "That's the last thing that we need right now."

"Colonel wants to meet with us in about an hour. All of us," said Stone.

"Now what's that supposed to mean?"

"I understand that we have a new lieutenant assigned to our office."

"Right."

"I haven't had the opportunity to meet her," said Stone, "though

I confess that I'm not looking forward to it."

"Now don't you start."

"Start what?" Stone asked innocently.

Price shook his head. "I wanted to get over to the morgue to talk with the doctors there."

Stone looked at his watch. "You've got about an hour before we have to meet the Colonel."

"Okay," said Price. "You go on to the office and tell Jackknife to pull everything we have on the alien planet, the asteroid, and anything else that seems to fit."

"Yes, sir."

"Wait," said Price. "Tell Monier to put down her impressions on everything. Have her rate the stuff according to her level of confidence in it."

"Yes, sir."

"I'll be along in a few minutes. I have a couple of questions that I want to get answered."

"Are they relevant?" asked Stone.

"Rocky, I don't believe that is a question that a sergeant should be asking a captain."

"Are they relevant?" repeated Stone, grinning.

"That I don't know. It's just something that I want to get answered before we take off."

"I'll get the others started," said Stone.

Price hesitated and then asked, "How big of a push is this going to be?"

"I think the Colonel has it in his mind to invade that planet but he wants some more information before he makes his decision."

"Okay. I'll see you in about thirty minutes."

Stone nodded and whirled, trotting down the corridor.

Price found Dr. James sitting in the brightly lighted morgue sipping coffee from a beaker in the time-honored tradition of all pathologists and lab workers. James was leaning back in his chair, his feet propped on his desk, looking as if he were fighting a losing battle with sleep.

"Dr. James?"

"Yes."

"The Colonel said that he would contact you so that you would answer all my questions on the autopsy of the alien," Price said.

James let his feet drop to the floor and set the beaker on his desk. "I've been informed by the Colonel to provide you with all information that you require."

"Good," said Price. Without waiting for an invitation, he dropped into the visitor's chair. "First, I want to know the cause of death."

James shrugged. "It didn't die."

"It's still alive?"

"No, it's dead, it just didn't die of natural causes or anything else."

Price shook his head and said, "I don't think I understand." And then suddenly he did. They had killed it. He felt his stomach turn over and his anger flare. There was a long-standing rule in intelligence and that was that a dead man could tell you nothing of value. They'd had an invaluable intelligence resource and then had subjected it to medical experimentation that had killed it.

"Whose brilliant idea was that?"

James shrugged again. "No one's really. We were trying to learn as much as we could and were subjecting it to medical examination. It didn't have the physical resources to survive."

"You assholes should have known that."

James raised his eyebrows but said reasonably, "Now why would we have known that? We had used ultra sound and MRI to examine the internal structure of the being. I will say that it was much simpler than I would have suspected."

Price almost didn't hear what was being said. He was still thinking about the timid creature that had revealed itself on the asteroid reluctantly. It hadn't wanted to leave its home until forced to do so by Price and his people.

"I would have thought," said Price, "that none of those things would kill it."

"They shouldn't have. We only wanted to know exactly how the creature had been put together and if its internal structure matched ours. It was not constructed to withstand any sort of rigorous examination surgery."

"Constructed?"

"Why yes," said James. "I thought you understood that. This being was not . . . a natural creature. It had been genetically engineered for the task that it had."

"You mean it wasn't sentient?"

"Strictly speaking it was. But it wasn't sentient in the sense that we humans are. It was a biological being with a small brain that had been programmed for a specific task. It was an artificial creature. It was not natural. It was apparently programmed to fulfill its task and then it expired."

"How did you figure that out?" asked Price.

"Studies on a cellular level," said James. "We were able to deduce this because of the lack of complexity of the internal structures and by examining the cellular material."

Price could think of several flaws in that thinking. Comparing an alien to a human to make such determinations didn't seem quite right to him, but he said nothing. Instead, he asked, "Then I take it the being was as vulnerable to our weapons as we are."

"Absolutely. Maybe more so simply because they don't have the internal mechanisms for repair that we have," said James, suddenly sounding like a professor lecturing a bunch of first-year students.

"I don't know, Doctor. I don't think we should have been experimenting on a creature from another world. Somehow it doesn't seem quite ethical."

"Well, I confess that I don't care what you think, Captain. I was told to answer your questions as completely as I could, but I don't have to listen to your moral philosophy. If you have another question, let's have it. If not, I've work to do." James stared at Price for thirty seconds and then turned his attention to his computer screen.

Price stood up, knowing that he'd scored a point with his criticism. James had gotten too angry too quickly. But he couldn't figure out why it had been important. Maybe it was simply to show up the scientists. They had experimented on a unique sample and destroyed it. That proved that they weren't infallible.

Holding out a hand, Price said, "Thank you, Doctor. Sorry about the judgmental comments."

James looked at Price's hand for a moment and then took it.

"Yeah . . . I am a little embarrassed by what happened. If you need anything else, please call."

"Sure. Thanks." Price couldn't think of anything else that he was going to need. He'd already gotten the answer. The Colonel had arranged it for some unknown reason.

CHAPTER 8

Standing on the deck in the hangar bay, wearing a close-fitting black outfit, Price felt foolish. Commandos from Earth about to infiltrate the enemy's position wore black outfits, painted their faces with camouflage paint, and wrapped their heads with bandanas that would keep the sweat out of their eyes. Intelligence officers on a ship in space didn't do that.

Next to him, Coollege and Monier were dressed in the same fashion. Near them, sitting on the deck, were their backpacks that contained everything they would need to survive their two days on the planet's surface. Readings from the surveillance computer on Clark's scout ship showed that they could live in the atmosphere though the oxygen content was slightly higher than Earth normal. Gravity was higher and the average temperature was higher. It was a hot, dry place but one on which they could survive.

Stone, dressed in a flight suit without insignia, was sitting on the deck, looking up under the ship. He was studying a hatch that didn't seem to fit properly. He slammed the heel of his hand into it, heard it pop into place, and said, "That's got it. No one touch it now."

"We about ready?" asked Price.

"Colonel coming down to say good-bye to us?" asked Stone.

"He did that at the staff meeting," said Price. "We're ready to go when you are."

"Then let's go. Are the scouts out yet?"

"Clark and his boys launched about two hours ago," said Price. "Everything is ready."

"Get your stuff stored, then," said Stone. "We'll get going in a few minutes."

Price picked up his pack, slung it over a shoulder, and moved to the rear of the ship. It was larger than a scout but smaller than a shuttle. It had a cockpit that could accommodate two pilots, a cargo bay that could carry six troopers and their assorted equipment, or enough gear, food, and ammunition for a platoon for the better part of a week.

The exterior was painted with a special coating that could, by the introduction of a magnetic field, change color so the ship could be used at night, high noon, land in a desert or in a dense green jungle. The camouflage could change to reflect its surroundings. And by creating variations in the magnetic field, it could also create a mottled pattern.

Price opened the side hatch, tossed his pack in, and then followed it. There wasn't much headroom. Price pushed his pack along the deck and then climbed up into one of the seats. He stored his gear, strapping it down so that it wouldn't shift under acceleration.

A moment later Coollege dropped into the seat opposite him. "I don't think I'm going to like this, Tree. They're sending us in again without a proper briefing."

"We have to go in to gather the data," said Price. "Then we can provide proper briefings for the others."

Coollege pointed. "What about her?"

"I have a name," said Monier.

"Don't mind Jackknife," said Price. "She's always difficult at the beginning of a mission, especially one where we don't have much in the way of information."

"I don't need you to apologize for me," she said.

"Or course you do," said Price. "Somebody has to point out that you're acting like a kid."

Coollege hitchhiked a thumb over her shoulder, indicating

Monier. "We don't know how she's going to react in a hostile environment."

"That's it," said Price. "We never know how the new guy is going to act on the first mission. Just drop it now. We all have to work together or we could all die." There was a silence and Price said, "Have I made myself clear on this? Do you understand me?"

Coollege didn't speak right away. Finally she said, "Yes, sir." She turned to Monier. "Sorry."

"No problem," said Monier.

Before anyone could say anything more, Stone said, over the intercom, "Let's get settled back there. Hatch secure?"

Monier looked at Price who said, "Use the lever to seal the door. Green light will tell you that it's sealed right."

Monier turned and did as she had been told. When she finished, she worked her way forward and took one of the remaining seats. As she belted herself in, she said, "I'm not getting much on this planet. There is something wrong there. I don't see any real danger . . . there seem to be people around, but there is something wrong with them."

"This is a great time to tell us," said Coolledge.

"I have a green board," said Stone on the intercom. "We will launch in two minutes. Let's get the gear stored and the seat belts fastened. There won't be another warning."

Price settled back and said, "We're going to have twenty hours before planetfall. We'll have plenty of time to review the data, if we think it necessary. I am satisfied with the briefing by the operations officer."

"This is not going into a planetary environment where the inhabitants are human. We don't blend in," said Coollege.

Price took a deep breath and exhaled. The arguments had already been made in front of the Colonel but he had decided that more information was needed. Something from the ground. Something that had a human imprint on it so that it could be done quickly without having to delay for computer orders and observations. Robots and computers were fine, but they didn't think for themselves and that was why Price and his people were now on the ship. Price could have explained this to Coollege but she had been told it all before. Debate was no longer needed. The orders had been issued.

"Survey said there were no people for us to worry about. We just observe, move around a little, and then Rocky picks us up. We don't have to concern ourselves with blending in. It'll be no sweat."

The ship moved, turned, and the view through the tiny window changed until Price could see the control room at the far end of the hangar deck. Behind the glass of the windows, people were working. Lights were flashing. They were preparing to launch one of the ships.

They slipped forward, slowly at first and then faster. The lights of the hangar bay disappeared and were replaced by the darkness of space. Price searched for stars that he recognized, but they were too far from Earth and without a base to work from, he couldn't be sure which star was which. The perspective was changed and the few constellations still recognizable weren't easily visible.

As soon as they were clear of the ship and the fleet they began a rapid acceleration. Looking out the window during the transition always made his head ache so he glanced back at Coollege. She was sitting bolt upright, her fingers gripping the armrests and her knuckles were pure white.

"Relax," he said.

"I hate to go to light speed. I just hate it."

Price said nothing. He waited, but there was nothing inside the cabin to tell them that the transition had been completed. Nothing to suggest they had burst through the light barrier. No change in sound, no bump or bounce, but when he looked out the window, the stars had changed color. It was the only way for him to be sure the transition had been made.

Monier leaned closer and said, "What do we do now?"

"We sit here and try to rest. We review the information we have. We eat as much as we can because once we're down, we can't worry about such things."

"Sounds like fun."

Clark was leading a half-dozen other scouts as they raced toward the planet. He watched the HUD, letting the numbers unwind as the distance between them and the planet disappeared.

He was searching for the pickets he'd found before. He, along with his flight, was to destroy them so that there would be no report of a ship entering the system. It was so the ship with the passengers could sneak in and out before it was discovered by anyone on the planet.

Clark didn't like this much more than he had liked being on the fleet ship. He hated being assigned as a flight leader. Now he was responsible for the other people in his flight. If he made a mistake, they could all die. That worried him a great deal but there was nothing he could do about it.

"Time to destination?" he asked the computer.

"Fifteen hours."

Clark nodded but he had known the answer. He'd been watching the chronometer since they had flashed away from the fleet. He had been dreading reaching his destination since then.

"Long-range scanners on."

"Acknowledged."

Now Clark concentrated on the HUD searching for signs of the enemy pickets. The system was still a couple of light-years distant and the signals from the scanners wouldn't reach it until long after Clark and the fleet had arrived. But, if there was something closer, a ship, a fleet, an asteroid, anything, the long-range scanner would find it for him. But the HUD was clean, displaying the readouts that were normal.

"If you detect anything, you advise me," said Clark.

"Acknowledged."

Clark snorted once. It was ridiculous to tell the computer to advise him. It would do that unless he reprogrammed it or shut it down. But Clark was afraid that he was going to miss something. To miss something would be to let the others with him down.

He tried to relax, to slip down in his seat to catch some sleep. When they reached the system he would have to be alert. But he couldn't sleep. His mind raced as he thought of the things that could go wrong, as he reviewed the various tactics that he would need as they approached the pickets . . . if there were pickets out there. Maybe there would be a fleet waiting for them and sweep them from the sky. He didn't know and the unknown scared him. That was new. Normally he delighted in that, but now there were others depending on him. It was his own fault. He had found the enemy and now he was paying the price for completing his mission successfully. He had been designated as the flight leader.

Monier crouched in front of Price and Coollege and said, "I just can't get much. There is something wrong here. Maybe it's the distance. I just don't know."

"How do we know this works?" asked Coollege.

Price shot her a glance, thinking of the argument about mind reading they'd had. Now Coollege was suggesting that Monier couldn't do it.

"I could give you a practical demonstration. We were selected after a series of tests. We were handed a sealed envelope and required to write a report on the contents without opening the envelope, of course. Another time we were required to provide reports on areas we'd never seen. A remote viewing they called it."

"Easy enough to say," said Coollege. "Especially after the fact."

"Jackknife," said Price, "you working on being an asshole? Let's just assume that somebody in command knows what he or she is doing. At the moment we have no reason not to believe in Monier's ability."

"Yeah. Right."

"Rachel," said Price, "tell us what you have."

"As I said. Not much. I get a feeling of coldness. A hardness about this place. It's not softened by human feelings or emotions."

"What about people?" asked Price.

"I don't know," she said. "Maybe the problem is the distance. I've never had that sort of trouble before, but then this is a whole new world. A whole new experience for me."

"You had a chance to explore the asteroid . . ."

"But there wasn't much there," said Monier. She closed her eyes and thought about that experience. There had been impressions but they seemed to be based not on what the builders had been feeling, but on the feelings of those who had been captured by it. The overwhelming impression had been one of fear or dread and that had been it. Nothing about the builders, the architects, the engineers, or the designers. Even when she had examined the crew compartment where the alien had slept there had been nothing. Just a relaxed feeling that indicated the being had slept most of the time it was on the asteroid, and they had already known that.

"Anything you can tell me would be very helpful," said Price.

"There is nothing to tell," said Monier.

"Now why am I not surprised?" asked Coollege.

"Shut up, Jackknife," said Price. "Just shut the fuck up."

"No," said Monier. "She's right. I haven't proved myself yet. I talk a good game but I haven't been able to produce anything that matters. Or anything that can be verified, which is the same thing."

"We still have some time."

"It won't do any good," said Monier. "If there is anything to get, I would have gotten it by now."

Price nodded and said, "Okay." He sat back in his seat and glanced to the right so that he could look out into space. There still was nothing to see. Only a scattering of stars looking blurred because they had shifted into light speed.

"Everyone understand the mission?"

"Tree, we all get it," said Coollege. "There is nothing for us not to understand. What's with you?"

That was the thing that Price didn't understand. He was nervous about this. Not the normal pre-insertion jitters, but a deeper fear because he knew so little about the enemy or the environment. On a regular mission they would have a historical connection to the enemy. Every mission had been to a planet inhabited by humans. Now there was nothing like that. There was no historical connection.

In fact, the problem went deeper because they had had a real intelligence source but it had been killed. That still bothered him. It would seem that any questions the biologists, the doctors, the physical anthropologists, or the pathologists had could have been answered with current technology without subjecting the creature to the tests that had apparently killed it.

Suddenly, Price realized that was exactly what bothered him. The pathologist saying that the creature had died as they tried to explore its internal structure. He wondered, briefly, if the creature hadn't been killed so that it wouldn't be able to answer the questions that he wanted answered.

"What's the matter, Tree?" asked Coollege.

"I don't like this mission."

"Well, join the club," said Coollege. "I've been saying that since the Colonel briefed us."

"It goes beyond that. I wish there was some way to call it off. I want it stopped."

"Getting chicken?" asked Coollege. She smiled as she said it to soften the criticism.

"No. Getting smart. If we can contact the scouts, I think we'd better call this off." He started to stand.

"You're kidding," said Coollege.

"No. I want some better answers before I'm dropped into an environment I don't understand. That we don't understand."

"Which is what I've been saying."

"Rachel," said Price, "there has to be some reason that your talent isn't working here. I don't want to do anything until I understand that problem a little better."

"You can't be considering a scrub based on that alone, can you?" she asked.

"No. There are some other problems as well." He leaned over and touched a button on the intercom. "Rocky, can we inform the scouts that we're going back to the fleet?"

"Are we?" asked Stone, his voice filled with surprise.

"If we can get the scouts recalled, I think we'd better. There are too many questions to be answered. The briefings and the planning for this mission have been inadequate."

"Give me a minute," said Stone. "I'll see if I can get a hold of them."

"Are you really authorized to scrub the mission?" asked Monier.

"Of course," said Price, suddenly relaxed. "At any point. As the mission commander, it is my responsibility to do so if the conditions warrant it."

Coollege breathed easier. "I didn't like this one either. Our preparation wasn't adequate."

"Yeah," said Price.

"Captain," said Stone. "Scouts are on radio silence. I can't recall them. There is no way for me to break through that without shielded, direct communication."

"Shit," said Price.

CHAPTER
9

There was a quiet chiming and a soft voice warned, "Contact. Contact. Contact."

"Put it on the HUD," said Clark.

The enemy was arranged in a straight, level line facing him. Four ships at the extreme range of the equipment with no IFF signals. It was obvious that these were not ships from any human source.

"Shielded signal to others in flight," said Clark.

"Signal sent and acknowledged."

"Time to maximum range for engagement and time to optimum range."

"One hour twenty minutes to maximum and two hours thirty-two to optimum."

Clark flipped a switch and used the shielded radio communications. "Scout flight, we will engage the enemy in about two hours. There will be no missile launches until orders are given. You may maneuver independently to protect your craft but let's maintain unit integrity as long as possible. Respond in scout order."

"Two."

"Three."

"Four."

"Five."

"Six."

To the computer, he said, "Show me the distribution of my scouts."

"In blue."

Clark studied the HUD. His ships were clustered near him while the enemy was spread over a wide area. That would change, he was sure. At the moment he wasn't going to order his group to spread to engage the enemy. They might tighten their formation later. If they remained spread, they could be taken one at a time. A six on one fight wouldn't last very long. If they clustered, the six on four odds still gave him the advantage.

Now he was searching for any change in the situation. Would there be more enemy ships appearing? Would they scatter? Did they even know that he was approaching with his flight? All these things would give him clues, but the enemy continued to patrol as he had, as if unaware that anyone was nearing.

The time slipped by as the enemy maintained his routine. They were boring holes in space, circling at the edge of their system. They took no notice of the approaching scouts.

"Scouts," said Clark finally. "Engaging closest enemy. Follow me in."

Clark took the control stick and put his left hand on the thruster controls. He aimed his ship at the enemy and then fired the first of his missiles. It flew straight and true. The enemy made no move to dodge the missile. Forty seconds after launch, the missile detonated. There was a bright flash and the first of the enemy ships was gone.

"Piece of cake."

"No unauthorized chatter," said Clark.

The rest of the enemy ships maintained their headings. Clark checked his instruments and found that there was no communication between the enemy ships. No electromagnetic radiation at all. Just a loose formation that continued to patrol as if nothing had happened.

"One, I am in range to attack."

Clark recognized the voice of William Carlson, one of the youngest of the scouts. "Four, hold your position."

"Roger."

Clark turned his scouts toward the second of the enemy ships. As he began the attack run, he said, "Six, break off and take out the farthest of the enemy."

"Roger."

"Four, you have the next."

"Roger."

"Five, you're with Six. Three, you're with Four. Two, you're on me. Respond in flight order."

"Two."

"Three."

"Four."

"Five."

"Six."

Now Clark focused on the enemy ship. He waited until he had a good lock and fired a single missile. Again, the enemy didn't try to evade. The missile slammed into the ship, detonated in a blinding flash of light, and was gone.

This bothered him. Why throw out pickets for sacrifice? Of course, with their disappearance, it would be obvious that something was happening. Sometimes that was the purpose of the pickets. They were out there to cause the enemy to announce themselves.

Watching the HUD, he saw the other enemy pickets disappear one by one. Scanning the space around them, he could see no evidence that there were any more enemy ships.

"Let's make the transmission that the first phase of the mission is complete."

There was a moment of silence and then, "Message sent and acknowledged."

"Good," said Clark.

"Our scouts have punched through the first line of defense of the enemy," said Stone over the intercom.

"Well," said Price, "I guess we're committed now."

"How long before planetfall?" asked Coollege.

"About an hour. Let's make our final check of the gear."

Monier pulled her pack from under her seat, opened it, and checked through it. She pulled out her pistol, held it up, and then slammed a magazine home. She set it on the seat beside her. "I'm ready."

"Don't chamber a round until we're on the ground."

"I've had enough training to know that we don't want the thing to fire in here," she said. "They did teach that much in the induction course."

Price touched each of the items in his pack as if to reassure himself they were real. He pulled his pistol out, checked it carefully, and then set it with a full magazine on the deck near his feet. He sometimes wondered why the command insisted on using the outdated weapons. The laser pistols and rifles, which could sometimes draw power from the environment depending on the circumstances, were considered too advanced. Until they knew what the level of the technology of the enemy was, they used the old stuff. It was effective, but it had resupply problems.

Coollege stood up and said, "I'll check the rifles and the grenade launcher."

Price raised an eyebrow in surprise. "Grenade launcher. I didn't request one."

"I did," said Coollege. "I don't like to leave these things to chance."

"Come on, Jackknife. A grenade launcher. Who's going to carry the ammo for it?"

"Ten rounds apiece. The ammo doesn't weigh all that much. It's no big thing."

"Okay," said Price, grinning.

As Coollege moved to the rear of the small cabin, Monier leaned close to Price. "What's she so paranoid about?"

"I think it has to do with training. She made a big deal of sneaking a jackknife on a survival mission once. Everyone thought it was great so now she tries to think of things that others overlook. The grenade launcher is the latest of her tricks."

"A grenade launcher could give us a very nice edge in some situations," said Monier.

"Not for a sneak and peak intelligence mission," said Price. "We're supposed to be subtle. There is nothing subtle about a grenade."

Coollege returned and said, "The rifles are ready. Ammo is next to them." She then slipped her pistol into a shoulder holster worn under her black clothing. She shifted the gear in her pack slightly, and then closed it up, checking the balance of it. She slipped it on her back, adjusted it until it was comfortable, and then took it off again.

"I'm ready," she said.

Price closed his pack and sat back. "At this point," he said, "I always feel there is something else that should be said, but I never know what it is."

"Then maybe we should just sit quietly, Tree," said Coollege.

"Maybe so."

The HUD was still clear and Clark couldn't help believing that he was flying into a trap. It was the old football play. Let the blitzing linebackers through so that they overran the play while the quarterback tossed a pass to a back with a screen of blockers. The key was to let the enemy through so that it could be neutralized.

But the HUD was clear. Nothing showed anywhere and unless the enemy's stealth capabilities were such that it could defeat all types of sensors, they should be able to spot them. Stealth was an outgrowth of military organizations and constant warfare. A society where there was no war would have no reason to develop stealth. The problem was that Clark didn't know if the enemy was warlike society or not. Their tactics, to this point, had been poor, but then, they did have weapons.

"We are entering the outskirts of their system," announced the computer.

Clark let the computer scan space all around him but the only thing that showed were his own ships. There was nothing else around them. Nothing of an artificial nature. No evidence of any equipment monitoring their progress.

"Where is the follow-up ship?" asked Clark.

"Gaining on us now," said the computer. "One hour behind."

Clark took a deep breath and rubbed a hand through his short-cropped hair. There was nothing for him to do but continue to push forward.

The line of scouts spread out along the elliptic plane. One of them broke off, diving toward a moon that was in a long orbit around the outermost planet.

Clark watched on the computer display fed back through shielded beam. He saw a dim surface covered with dust, ice crystals, and impact craters. The diving scout, cameras running, made a low orbit of the moon, found nothing radiating, and lifted up, back into space. He had been searching for some kind of outpost and found nothing.

"Moon is clean."

"Roger, Six."

The computer said, "No readings on the outer planets. No detectable radiation. Ninety-four percent probability that there are no outposts present on this planet or any of the moons orbiting it."

As the scouts fanned out, across the system, they continued toward the fourth planet. Clark kept his eyes on the HUD and the sensors, watching for any indication that the enemy knew that they were coming.

As they neared the target planet, the line began to contract again so that the scouts were in a loose formation no more than half a klick across. They had turned off all their lights, radios, radars, and engines so that they were emitting nothing for the enemy to detect. They slipped forward in silence, heading for the large city that dominated the north pole of the planet.

The computer said, "Secondary craft is now fifteen minutes from touchdown."

The sound of the computer's voice seemed unnaturally loud to Clark. He almost told it to shut up and then realized that it wouldn't shut up and that the enemy would never be able to detect the sound anyway.

He looked out the tiny window. The planet dominated his view. The city was a dung-colored expanse on the top of the world. He had no real mission, other than buzz the city and keep it busy watching him and his scouts for a few minutes. Let it detect a lot of activity in the sky and hope that it didn't bother to monitor the rest of the planet's surface.

"Secondary craft is ten minutes from touchdown."

Clark turned on his radio, unshielded, and ordered, "Let's begin the run. Respond in flight order."

"Two."

"Three."

"Four."

"Five."

"Six."

Clark turned on his lights and radars, boosting the power levels so that he would suddenly burst into prominence. It would appear that a ship exploded on any electromagnetic detectors below. It should draw all attention to him and his scout flight.

He pushed the stick over and punched through the upper reaches of the atmosphere. There was a shuddering, as if he had flown into a thunderstorm, but it dampened out quickly. He steepened the dive.

"Activate all sensors."

"Tracking of our ship," said the computer.

They were plummeting toward the surface. Clark was watching as the radar altimeter unwound rapidly. He kept an eye on the HUD and a hand on the thrusters.

"Missile launch," announced the computer.

That was what Clark had been waiting for. He pulled back on the stick, worked the thrusters, and waited for the nose to come up. "Where is the missile?"

"Missile on the right, forty-two thousand feet below, accelerating rapidly."

"Type of homing?"

"Radar lock."

"Pop a chaff dispenser."

"Chaff fired."

Clark rolled to the right, dove slightly, and then jinked right and left trying to break the radar lock. He watched the HUD, seeing that the missile had finally locked onto the chaff cloud. It popped through chaff and then detonated in a boiling, roiling burst of bright orange fire and dense black smoke.

Clark felt relieved. It had been simple to defeat the missile. "Status of other scouts."

"In line, diving on target."

"Status of secondary mission."

"Ship has disappeared."

To himself, Clark said, "I hope they made it in."

CHAPTER 10

"The one thing that I can never decide," said Price, "is if we should go in with our seat belts buckled or unbuckled. If the area is hot, then we want to get out as quickly as possible. But if something should go wrong on the landing, we'd want to be belted in for our own protection."

"Unbuckled," said Coollege. "If we crash, we're probably not going to be in very good shape even if belted in. Besides, the enemy will probably kill us anyway."

"Thank you for that delightful thought," said Price sarcastically. He realized that he was talking now because he was nervous. He was always nervous before a landing even if he knew everything that he needed to know for survival. Any mission did that to him.

Monier was leaning over, pushing at her pack. She straightened up and said, "I'm ready."

Price was struggling to get his pack shouldered. He adjusted it until it was fairly comfortable and buckled his pistol belt. Then, shifting the pack slightly, he tightened down the shoulder straps.

"You're not ready until you've got your pack on," Coollege told Monier. "If something happens and we have to scramble

78

out of the aircraft you will leave behind everything that is not fastened to your body."

"Of course," said Monier.

Over the intercom, Stone said, "We're about to enter the atmosphere. Let's be alert."

"Have they spotted us?"

"No indications of it. Scouts are still harassing the Citadel."

"Citadel?" said Price.

"That big city area at the top of the world," said Stone.

"How long until we touch down?"

"About twelve minutes. I've got everything set passive. We haven't been detected, as far as I can tell."

"Keep me advised."

"Roger that."

Price leaned back in his seat and wiggled, trying to get comfortable with the pack on his back. He reached down and tried to buckle the seat belt but it wouldn't adjust enough so that he could still sit there.

Coollege brought him one of the rifles and handed it to him, along with a bandolier that held a dozen spare magazines for it. He draped the bandolier over his head and shoulder so that it was hanging across his chest.

"Ten minutes," said Stone. "No indications that the enemy is aware of us."

"Monier?" asked Price.

She closed her eyes and then shrugged. "I'm getting nothing. No hostile vibrations out there. If they know we're coming, they don't care."

"Crap," said Coollege.

"Once on the ground," said Price, "we get out quickly and get away from the ship. Stone's got to take off as fast as he can. We don't want to expose him to hostile fire if we can avoid it."

"Sure, think of him," said Coollege.

"And if he gets out, he's no longer a beacon that leads right back to us," said Price.

"Right," said Coollege.

"Once on the ground," said Monier, "what are we going to do?"

"Get away from the landing zone as quickly as we can," said

Price. "If the enemy is monitoring, they might know that we landed. If they want to search, that would be the place to start it."

"Yeah," said Monier.

"Five minutes," said Stone.

Price put a magazine into his rifle, slapped the bottom to seat it, and then worked the bolt, looking down into the breech to make sure the first round was seated properly. He wished again they could have brought the laser rifles. No problem with ammunition. No worry about an accidental discharge as long as the battery pack was unplugged.

"Everyone set?" asked Price.

"Set," said Coollege. She was sitting calmly on the edge of her seat, her backpack forcing her forward.

Monier looked scared. Her face was drained of color. Her fingers danced over her rifle, touching the trigger guard, the bolt, the barrel, as if trying to make sure that all the parts were still there. She looked up suddenly, her eyes wide, and said, "Set."

Coollege hitchhiked a thumb at Monier. "If she's psychic, how come she's so scared?"

"Shut up, Jackknife," said Price.

"It's okay," said Monier.

"No, it's not. If we're going to work together on this, we have to trust one another."

Coollege nodded slightly and said, "Sorry."

"No," said Monier. "I don't blame you. It is a radical concept."

"Two minutes," said Stone.

"Here we go," said Monier.

Price laughed and said, "I don't care how often I do this or how small the team is, someone always says that."

"Sorry."

"Brace yourselves," said Stone.

Price leaned back in the seat, his hands on the arms, and waited. Monier had her eyes closed and her lips were moving as if she was praying silently. Coollege was looking toward the window but there was nothing to see except the darkness of night. No lights to break up the landscape, nothing traveling on the ground, and nothing coming up to intercept them.

"About a minute. You'll know when we're down. Get out as quickly as you can."

No one in the rear answered. The lights had been turned down to a red glow that was just bright enough so that Price could see the outlines of the others. Their faces took on a strange look in the dull red light.

They bounced once and then dropped sickeningly, like an elevator that was falling free. They bottomed out, hit the ground, and bounced again. Price lost his grip on the arms of the seat and fell to the deck. He rolled to the bulkhead and tried to sit up.

"You okay?" asked Coollege.

"Yeah."

They stopped suddenly, as if they had run into something solid. The rear of the ship lifted and then dropped. Monier fell forward landing on her face. She grunted as she hit the deck.

As soon as they stopped, Price leapt up. He shook his head as if to clear it. He worked his way toward the rear door and bent low to twist the locking wheel.

Coollege joined him. "Hurry."

Price spun the wheel and pulled in and lifted up. The door slipped out of the way. "Go."

Coollege jumped down, onto the soft ground, not even thinking about the fact that she was the first human to set foot on the planet. She stumbled and put out a hand to stop her fall.

Price saw Monier and said, "Hurry."

She reached the door and dropped through. Price followed her, turned, and pulled at the door so that he could close it. He heard the quiet clicks as it locked.

"Jackknife? Where are you?"

"Here."

Price saw Monier crouched near the rear of the ship. He reached down and grabbed her under the arm. He pulled her to her feet. "Let's get moving."

She stumbled forward and then stopped. She looked back, confused.

Price pushed her toward a black smudge in the distance. "We'll head for those trees."

"Where's Coollege?"

"Over there. Come on, we've got to move."

Behind them there was a single flash of light and then a roar began building. The ship lifted like a helicopter and spun to the right until it was facing the direction from which it had come.

"Rocky's going to take off. We've got to get clear."

At that moment Monier disappeared from sight. Price glanced down and spotted her lying at the bottom of a ditch. He jumped in and as he did, the engines of the ship roared as it lifted off. At five hundred feet it turned away from them, changing from a large black craft into a bright burning fire. The nose came up and the roar became deafening as the ship shot higher into the atmosphere. In seconds it had faded from sight.

"Tree?"

Price stood up. Through the tall grasses and low bushes he could see Coollege moving. She was crouched over, bent at the waist like a woman fighting a strong wind.

"Get to the trees," he said quietly. "We're right behind you."

She turned and began to lope across the field, running toward the trees in the distance. She vanished in the darkness.

"Come on," said Price. He climbed from the ditch and knelt in the thick grass. It was a dry, brittle grass that rattled as he moved.

Monier stood up and reached out for a hand. Price took it and hauled her up. He pointed toward the trees and said, "Run in that direction. Coollege is waiting."

"Okay," she said but she didn't move immediately. Instead she seemed to stare at the trees, moving her face back and forth like a radar antenna searching for the enemy. "Nothing out there in front of us."

"Then move it," said Price.

Monier got to her feet and began to jog across the field like she was trying to burn off calories. She did not resemble a military officer on a mission but a long-distance runner on a track.

"Amateur," he said. He waited until she was about halfway to the trees and then started after her. He kept low, using the shadows for cover.

As he got close to the trees, he slowed and then stopped short. He listened to the sounds around him. He'd been on dozens of planets and there had always been background noise. Insects buzzing, small engines, animals, or people. Here there was nothing. Only the same quiet that he'd heard in the isolation chamber.

"Tree?"

Price didn't answer. He stood up and began to work his way into the trees.

Clark was watching the progress of the attack on the HUD. Scout Two had rolled through, fired a single missile that had been engaged and destroyed by a single energy beam. A laser beam had stabbed out, touched the ship, and then slipped off. Scout Two's tail glowed brightly for an instant and then it began to cool.

"Three is rolling in."

Clark punched a button and the screen to the left brightened, showing him a rear view. "Magnification ten on the left."

"Acknowledged."

Now he could see the third scout ship as it dove from the outer reaches of the atmosphere. It was a streak of brightness that was aimed right at the center of the Citadel. It began to glow from the friction of the dive.

Clark took his eyes off the screen, scanned the HUD and the sky outside. There was nothing to see either on the screen or in the atmosphere.

Scout Three fired one missile but as it dropped from the rail, it exploded. A beam from the city had touched it. The detonation flipped the scout ship over. Fire burst along the side. It flashed toward the tail, whipped by the speed of the craft through the air.

The pilot twisted the ship around, spinning, trying to put out the fire but that didn't work. Then he righted his ship, shallowed the dive but the flames stuck to the hull. It began to glow cherry-red.

"Three is in trouble."

"Four, stick with him," said Clark.

"Four, roger."

Scout Three tried to climb then, but the ship didn't respond to the controls. Flames had melted the thruster ports. He was stuck.

"Three is going down."

"Four is with you."

"Five, begin the run. Six, you're with him."

"Five."

"Six."

"Two, join on me," said Clark.

"Two."

Three slipped lower, closer to the Citadel. There was nothing he could do to put out the fire. Instead, he dumped the nose, aimed at the Citadel, and punched off everything he carried. Missiles flashed and streaked. Four bombs tumbled free, falling toward the center of the city. The sudden decrease in weight lifted the craft and the nose came up. But the fire continued to burn.

Below beams flashed, targeting each of the missiles and the bombs. They exploded one by one in brilliant flashes. The display lasted for only seconds. Then came a final detonation as Scout Three disintegrated.

"We lost Three. We lost Three!"

Clark didn't respond. He'd seen it explode on the screen but that had been unreal, like watching one of the holos he used on long missions. It was something created for his entertainment.

The call from Two woke him from it. The panic and awe in the voice made the death of the pilot real. He thought that he should say something but there were no words.

The Citadel wasn't finished. Now it had learned that the attack could be stopped. Beams from all over the surface stabbed up looking like a thousand multicolored searchlights. They scanned across the sky.

"Let's get out of here," said Clark. It was apparent that they had the attention of the Citadel. It was trying to sweep them from the sky.

Scout Four was hit by one beam and tried to twist away. A second focused on it and then a third. The hull began to superheat and the metal of the skin started to run like water. One of the beams punched through to the electronics, frying the computer. The HUD popped and darkened. The flight instruments failed, then the flight controls. But that didn't matter. A second beam holed the rear and destroyed the engines. The craft then blew up.

Scout Five ceased to exist a moment later. The rear blew off and the nose cartwheeled forward. A small portion separated, a rocket fired, propelling it away from the burning, tumbling wreckage.

"Five got out," said Six. The relief in his voice was unmistakable.

A beam followed the pod and an instant later it was gone. The escape pod disintegrated without a flash or detonation. It just ceased to exist.

"Scouts, this is Lander. We're out."

Clark keyed the mike. "Scouts. Let's go." He hit the thrusters and was thrown back in his seat. He looked at the HUD to watch the Citadel recede but it wasn't happening fast enough. The beams were still reaching for him, dancing across the hull of his ship. And then he was suddenly clear of the atmosphere.

"Scout check."

"Two."

"Six."

Half his force was gone. He hoped that it had been worth the price.

CHAPTER

11

Price crouched in the darkness, his hand on the smooth bark of a tree trunk. It was so dark in the forest that Price couldn't see anything other than the black shape of the tree and a single bush about two feet from him. Overhead, through a break in the canopy, he thought he could see a small portion of the night sky. He knew that Coollege and Monier were in the forest somewhere but he couldn't actually see them.

"We can't travel through this, Tree," said Coollege softly. She was to his right.

"We could drop back and skirt the edge of the woods," said Price. "At least we could see one another."

"Standard procedure says that we travel across the worst possible terrain and at night or in bad weather."

"Doctrine doesn't mean squat here," said Price. "Besides, that's escape and evasion."

"If I might interrupt," said Monier. "I'm getting nothing here. Anywhere around here. I think it would be safe for us to travel outside the woods."

"There," said Price, suddenly speaking in a normal tone of voice. "See?"

That surprised and shocked Coollege. "Be quiet, Tree," she said.

"Why? Rachel says we're all alone."

"If we believe her."

"I do," said Price. "Which way should we go?"

Monier was quiet for a moment and then pointed. "In that direction." Her hand was barely visible. Price had located her by the sound of her voice.

"I can't see anything over there," said Coollege.

"Rachel, you have the point. Walk very carefully, slowly. We're not interested in getting very far, just that we make some progress."

"Sure, Tree."

"She's got the point?" asked Coollege incredulously.

"She can *see* better than either of us." Price stood up and stepped closer. He reached out, feeling for Monier with his left hand. He touched the top of her head. "Let's go. I'll hold on to your shoulder. Jackknife, you need to hang on to me."

"Right."

Monier was on her feet, facing away from them. "I just walk along?"

"Slowly," said Price. "Using a walking stick to feel your way along. We don't want to go strolling off a cliff."

"Walking stick?"

"Stay right here," said Price. He let go of her and worked his way around, feeling with his right hand. He found a sapling, crouched, and cut it off near the ground with his knife. He stripped the tiny branches and the leaves from it quickly. He turned and stared into the darkness and no longer had any idea where Coollege and Monier were. He couldn't see them though he knew that he was no more than a few feet from them.

"Somebody is going to have to say something."

"Right here, Tree," said Coollege. She sounded as if she were disgusted with him.

He turned his head toward the sound and walked into Monier. She stumbled back but Price caught her before she could fall. "Sorry."

Coollege reached out and touched him. "If we're through clowning around."

Price ignored her. He handed the walking stick to Monier. "Don't hurry. We have all the time we need." He felt Coollege's hand on his shoulder. He glanced back but even though she was in arm's reach, she was little more than an indistinct charcoal smudge.

Monier probed the ground in front of her with the stick and found it to be solid. She lifted the stick, swung it right and left, searching for something she might walk into, and then took a step. She began to work the stick rapidly. Right, left, probe to the front, and then a couple of steps.

The system worked fine until she walked into a low-hanging branch. She bumped her head and grunted in surprise and pain. She stopped walking.

"What?" asked Price.

"Bumped my head."

"Some psychic," said Coolledge.

Price felt Monier stop. There was a tension in her shoulders that hadn't been there a moment ago. He could feel her turn her head.

"I've about had it with you," she said, her voice low and filled with fury. "You don't have a clue about what you're talking about."

"I know that you're not trained for this. We've got to carry you."

"Knock it off," said Price, suddenly angry. Arguments on the ship were one thing but on the planet's surface they were something else. "There will be no more discussion of this. Period. We have got to work together or the mission is as good as finished."

"I wasn't searching for branches. I'm trying to find intelligence around here," said Monier anyway.

"Right," said Coollege.

Price let his hand drop from Monier's shoulder and turned to face Coollege. He still could not see her, but could feel her hot breath on his face.

"You are supposed to be a professional. Act like it."

"Yes, sir!"

Price was going to say more but stopped. He knew that Coollege was just reacting. She'd figure it out in a moment. They had to work together regardless of feelings. He turned and put his hand on Monier's shoulder. "Let's go."

They started off again, ducking under the branch that Monier had found. Now, she worked the stick quickly but held a hand up feeling for more low-hanging branches. She stared into the dark, trying to see anything that might be in her path.

With her mind she reached out, beyond the woods and into the areas ahead of them, toward the major city. She knew there was something close. Small and furry with almost no intelligence. A small animal that operated on instinct rather than cunning. That was the thing. She could pick up impressions from the higher animals. Feelings of fear, caution, hunger, and some emotions. Dogs were often happy to see a friendly face. Chimpanzees actually thought about problems and could work with other chimps to solve them. But here the animal reading was very low level and she could only pick up the single individual. She put that out of her mind.

As she felt around with her mind, she realized that the hand on her shoulder was reassuring. She didn't know if Price was trying to calm her or if he had the confidence in her that he seemed to be radiating. It didn't matter. She appreciated the feeling.

She slowed then and stopped. Price leaned close and whispered, "What?"

"We're about to exit this part of the forest."

"Wait one," said Price. He slipped to one knee and listened carefully.

Coollege, right behind him, turned so that she was facing back the way they had come. She was watching to make sure that no one came up on them, though it would be next to impossible for her to see them in the darkness.

"I'm going to check this out," said Price, now being quiet, whispering in Coollege's ear.

She didn't answer him. Suddenly they were a team again, in a hostile environment. Extra noise could lead the enemy right to them.

Price worked his way forward slowly, one hand out in front of him. He moved with a precision that was built on all his training. He noticed that the forest was becoming lighter in front of him. The trees weren't as tall and the foliage not as thick.

He reached the end of the forest and stopped. It looked as if a giant had taken a knife and sliced off the trees at that point. It was a straight line. Beyond it was an empty field. Price couldn't tell if it was a cultivated field, a park, or something else. It was still too dark for him to see anything useful.

He stretched out on the ground and studied the area. He listened but there was still no sound, other than a quiet rustling caused by a light breeze. But still there were no insects, animals, birds, or even the noise of civilization. It was as if there was nothing but the vegetation.

Slipping to the rear, he stood and moved back into the forest, scanning right and left, but still unable to see anything other than the blackness of the forest. "Jackknife."

"Here."

"Again," said Price.

"Right here."

Price moved toward the sound and saw the hunched shape of Coollege on the ground. She was moving her hand back and forth so that it would be easier for him to see her.

"Let's rest here for a few minutes. We've got a large field to cross before the sun comes up."

"How long until that?" asked Coollege.

Price pulled back the long sleeve of his camouflage jacket and realized that ship time, based on Earth time, had no relevance to the planet.

"Couple of hours, I think. I don't know."

"Shouldn't we eat something?" asked Monier.

"Not yet," said Price. "Drink some water if you want but we won't eat until after we find a place to hole up for the day."

"Okay," she said, but she didn't understand it. There would be no one searching for them. She was sure of that.

Clark had formed his scouts in a loose formation on his ship as they had flashed from the planet's atmosphere. He kept checking the HUD, hoping that the missing ships would reappear though he knew they wouldn't. They were gone. He'd seen them explode under the focused attention of the planet's point defense system.

His computer was scanning space ahead of him and had found nothing there. Behind him were a number of small ships, but all had been identified as the landing ships launched from the fleet. A half-dozen intelligence teams had been inserted. Now those ships were off the planet's surface and all were racing to join on him.

He knew that the destruction of half his flight was not his fault. It was the breaks of the game but he still felt responsible. There should have been something that he could have done to prevent the loss. That thought kept intruding though he tried to ignore it. Now was not the time to dwell on those problems. That was something that would come later. Now he had to get clear of the enemy's system.

"Approaching edge of planetary system," said the computer.

Clark checked the HUD again. The flight was joined with no stragglers. Sensor sweeps had shown nothing in front of him. The enemy wasn't waiting to ambush them.

Over the radio, he said, "Prepare for jump to light speed on my mark."

There was a series of acknowledgments. Clark then touched a series of buttons, flipped a switch, and said, "Let's go to light speed."

As the ship transited the barrier, Clark sank back into his seat. He kept his eyes moving from instrument to instrument but that was only something to occupy his mind. He kept slipping back, watching his own run on the Citadel as if he were outside his ship, waiting for the enemy to respond. Then he could see the others as they rolled in, trying to light the sky with a display that would keep the attention of anyone on the ground. Here was the extraterrestrial menace over their city. Keep them busy while the other ships slipped in far to the south to land the intelligence teams.

"It was a stupid plan," he said out loud. It wouldn't have fooled them for a minute. They would have been able to see the invaders over the pole and the others trying to sneak in even if they were coming in low from another direction. Who had thought it would work?

And then he realized it had worked because the ships had landed and had gotten away. All the teams were in place, moving on toward the Citadel. It had cost three scouts, but they had gotten down.

"Flight integrity intact after jump to light," the computer told him.

"Time to fleet?"

"Nineteen hours."

"Nineteen hours," repeated Clark. He wanted to be there now. He wanted to go through the debriefing, talk about what he'd seen, review the computer logs and holo record, and get it over with. That was what he wanted.

The radio crackled and Clark heard, "Scouts, well done."

That was it, the whole message. Clark recognized the voice of the Colonel. He was violating procedure to let them know that the sacrifice had been appreciated.

Out loud, Clark said, "Bullshit."

The field wasn't much different from the one they had landed in several hours earlier. The vegetation was about knee high. The field was level without any ditches or rocks or hills. Just a flat plain, not unlike a cultivated field, though the crops hadn't been planted in rows and from the tangle at the base of them, it didn't seem that anyone cared much about agriculture. The field had been leveled and that was all that Price could tell about it.

Off on the horizon there was a light band of pink that faded to gray and rose toward the zenith. If they had been on Earth, Price would have called it east . . . and since direction was an arbitrary designation, he decided that it was the east.

Coollege, who had been about five feet behind him, stepped closer and whispered, "Sun's going to rise."

"I can see."

"Looks like the trees are about a mile away. We're not going to make it before daylight."

"I don't think it matters," said Price.

Monier, still in the lead, had tossed away the walking stick. She was moving rapidly, her head down as she looked at the ground.

Price scanned the horizon. It was definitely brighter than it had been. The charcoal-grays had brightened, lightening so that shapes were now visible. All he could see were bushes and trees. Nothing to suggest that the planet was inhabited.

Coollege was staying close now. "You don't think Rocky put us on the wrong planet, do you?"

"Rocky landed us right where we're supposed to be. That doesn't mean that somebody else didn't screw up."

"This is great."

The trees were closer but they were also brighter. Price noticed that the leaves looked more like cotton candy that had been painted green and glued to the trunks. He was sure that he would see a split rail fence when the sun was finally up. But as they approached the other end of the field and the ground became lighter, it was obvious that there would be no fence.

Monier stopped just before she entered the trees. She turned and looked back at Price. He waved her forward and she disappeared.

"This is the strangest assignment I've ever had," said Coollege as they neared the trees.

"Search for an enemy that doesn't seem to exist," said Price.

"Long before we jumped into space," said Coollege, "we had filled our planet with cities, factories, and farms."

They entered the trees. Monier had stopped and was standing near a large bush covered with yellow flowers. She was covered in sweat and looked tired. "I think we need to rest."

Price nodded. "Let's take a couple of hours. Eat something. Get some sleep. You picking up anything?"

"Nothing at all."

"Strangest planet I've ever seen."

CHAPTER
12

They couldn't hold the briefing in the normal conference room because there were too many people who were going to be involved. All the pilots from the various missions, the staff officers, and the intelligence officers were also there. And the Colonel had also invited a number of infantry officers from other regiments to attend the meeting. It was going to be the planning session.

The room was as noisy as a theater before the play started. Dozens were talking, speculating, shouting greetings at friends they hadn't seen for days and then disagreeing with the orders they knew would be issued. When the hatch irised open and the Colonel stepped through, the room fell silent, almost as if a switch had been thrown.

The Colonel moved to the front of the room, near the control panel for the holo and computer. There was a large, high-backed leather chair waiting for him. A sergeant stood waiting for the Colonel, holding a leather folder that contained all the information that had been gathered.

The Colonel sat in the chair, waved a hand, and said, "Let's be seated."

There was a rustling as the men and women sat down, but no

one spoke. They waited to learn what was happening, though many of them had heard various rumors.

"As you know," said the Colonel without preamble, "a number of months ago we discovered an asteroid traveling between stars. It was an artificial construct filled with scientific experiments and equipment. Obviously, this was the result of an intelligence that had launched the craft long before we had developed any type of civilization, let alone space travel."

The air above the audience, which was sitting in rows facing the Colonel, shimmered and a holo of the asteroid drifted over them, rotating slowly to give everyone a good view of the entire craft.

"Scout searches for the last several months were unsuccessful in locating the home planet. Recently, Randly Clark changed all that. We have located the home world of the builders of the asteroid. We have inspected their world and have landed six intelligence teams on it."

The Colonel waited for a burst of noise, but the staff sat in dead silence. Some of them were watching the rotating orb in front of them. Others had focused their attention on the Colonel as he stood there.

The scene above the stage changed slowly. The silvery orb faded away, replaced by a light brown planet with a tan cap to it. The large oceans were a bright blue and there were even a few clouds hovering over the planet to make it look more realistic.

"As we approached this planet, our scouts were attacked. Lieutenant Clark engaged them, punched through their picket line, and explored the planet. He was engaged by their defensive systems. When we put down the intell teams, Clark and his scouts were again attacked." The Colonel looked at Clark. "That's right, isn't it?"

"Yes, sir."

"Now, I think we can assume that the inhabitants of the planet are hostile."

One of the staff officers held up a hand and said, "Sir, I don't think we can assume these people are hostile without a little more data."

"They shot down three of our scouts," said the Colonel evenly.

"After we shot our way into their system. I venture to say we would react with hostility if the situation were reversed," said the officer.

"Captain," said the Colonel, "we are not here to debate the situation. Those decisions have already been made."

"Yes, sir."

Without waiting for more, the Colonel flipped a page in his notebook and began to talk. He gave them all the information that had been learned since the asteroid had been captured. He told them about the other aliens who had also managed to enter it but who had died before they could learn the secrets of it. He talked of the studies that provided clues about the location of the builder's home world. He talked of the many recons by scouts and the building of a base of information until they knew as much as they could without having anyone to spy on the planet's civilization.

"That is all changing," said the Colonel. "We now have teams on the planet's surface searching for answers to these questions. They are in communication with our intelligence facilities remaining here on the flagship."

One of the infantry officers looked up and said, "Are we going to invade . . . on the ground?"

"That is the question we're here to answer."

Price had left Monier and Coollege behind, hidden under the large flowering bush. Monier slept while Coollege kept her eyes open, searching for anything that didn't belong. Price had crawled away, first deeper into the woods, but when it looked as if there would be no break in the forest for a long distance, he turned and headed for the open field. He wanted a view of the sky and the distance. He wanted to see if there was life, intelligent life, anywhere on the planet.

As he neared the edge of the forest, he could see the light bleeding in. He got down on his stomach and crawled forward slowly, being careful not to make noise. It wasn't that he believed there was anyone around to hear him, or to see him, it was his training. He'd been taught to follow the procedures even when it seemed those procedures would do nothing to enhance the mission. It was when procedure was ignored that disaster happened.

He reached the edge of the forest. His impression from the night hadn't been wrong. It looked as if the forest had been cut away in a straight line. But the field didn't hold a crop. It was a tangle of green, red, and yellow vines, bushes, and grasses. There was a waving line of taller, brown grass off to one side and he suspected that marked the course of a stream or maybe some kind of drainage ditch.

He lay at the edge of the forest, in the shadow of a large tree with a greenish trunk. He didn't know if the color was the result of a fungus or if the bark was naturally green. Lying next to it, he still couldn't tell.

There was no movement anywhere around him except for a gentle waving of the grass in the light breeze. Nothing flew over the field. No birds or insects were anywhere around.

Normally, in a forest, there would be the calls of birds, the cries of animals, and the scramble of tiny claws on the trees, rotting vegetation, and the wood. Here there was nothing. No sound at all.

He watched the sky overhead, assuming that if there was anything to see, it would be there. Maybe a high-flying plane. Maybe a helicopter or small aircraft of some kind. There was nothing other than some strange-colored clouds. They looked muddy.

Satisfied that there was nothing to see, Price pushed himself away from the edge of the forest. He stood up and walked, naturally and unhurriedly, back to the bush where Coollege and Monier waited for him.

He got to his hands and knees and crawled under the bush. Coollege was sitting with her back against the thick trunk. She was sipping water and blinking rapidly. "Something is stinging my eyes," she said quietly.

In a normal tone of voice, Price said, "Probably something given off by the flowers."

"Should you be talking out loud like that?"

"There is nothing around here. Nothing at all. I think we're wasting our time. I think we should make tracks for the city and not worry about anything else."

"SOP," said Coollege.

"Is designed as a guideline and not as orders to be followed without modification."

"Yes, sir."

Monier stirred, rolled to her side, and stretched, seeming to forget where she was. She said, "What in the hell . . ." And then she remembered.

"Are you getting anything?"

Monier closed his eyes and fell silent. After a moment she said, "I can detect nothing other than us. Nothing at all. Not even insects."

"You can read insects?" asked Coollege.

"I can detect them. I can't read them. I can't read you either. I can get impressions."

"Nothing around?" said Price.

"No."

Price sat down and crossed his legs. He was hunched slightly, ducking under a branch heavy with flowers. He reached up to push it away and felt a sudden stinging in his eyes. He blinked rapidly and looked away.

"Defense mechanism," said Monier.

"Now she's going to tell us that she can read plants."

"Electrical signals transmitted by them," she said. "Same as with insects. Electrical activity . . . there are plants on Earth that . . ."

"We don't need a lecture here," said Price.

"Yes, sir."

Price looked at his watch. It gave him a frame of reference, even if it meant nothing on this planet. "I want to get moving. We have a lot of territory to explore."

"Message to fleet?"

"Nothing to report."

Coollege nodded, pulled a small hand-held radio from her pack. She touched the keypad, put in the message, and then asked, "Is that it?"

"Yeah . . . wait. Tell them that we have found no sign of animal life. Plant life but no animals or insects."

"Is that important?" asked Monier.

Price shrugged. "In intelligence everything might be important."

"Data loaded and ready for burst transmission."

"Go ahead."

"Message off."

"Already?" asked Monier.

"A burst transmission of a nanosecond," said Price, "is nearly impossible to detect."

"Oh."

Coollege had finished repacking the radio. "I'm ready to go."

Price hesitated and then shook his head. "Monier, you have the point again. Straight north, toward the city. Steady pace. Stay under cover and if you come to an open area, you halt. If you pick up any unidentified readings, you halt. If you don't understand something, you halt."

"Yes, sir."

"Why does she have the point again?" asked Coollege.

"Because she has the best chance of spotting an ambush if there is one."

"Sure."

"Let's go," said Price.

The Colonel listened to the debate among the staff officers as they argued about the best method of invading the planet. He watched as they studied the Citadel that sat atop the world, viewing it from every angle using the limited data provided by the scouts and enhanced by the ship's computers.

The hatch irised open once and as it did, everyone in the room fell silent. As soon as the hatch was closed, they all began to talk again. The woman came forward, leaned close to the Colonel, and said, "Preliminary reports from all intell teams have been received."

The Colonel looked up into her eyes. "What is it?"

She raised an eyebrow. "All negative."

"Now what in the hell does that mean?"

"None of the teams found anything to report. Two of them mentioned there was no animal life encountered. One said there were no insects. One mentioned there were no roads or railways as far as they could see. Another said no cultivated fields though it appeared the forests had been modified by genetic engineering or by simple cross-breeding."

"That tells me exactly nothing," said the Colonel.

"That's all there is. All teams reported in and no team reported any type of trouble. All reported on schedule and there was no interference from outside sources. All are continuing to make their way toward the Citadel."

"All right. Thank you." He was quiet for a moment and then asked, "Oh, has the General seen this?"

"Yes, sir. He said for you to continue with the briefing. Final decision will be made based on the next reports from the intell teams."

"Thank you."

The woman left and the Colonel watched the debates continue. Finally he stood up and said, "Let's get something organized."

"Any word from the teams on the surface?" asked one of the officers.

"They have negative contact. Nothing. Apparently the only life exists around the Citadel." He held up a hand and added, "That is what they report at the moment."

"Then this should be simple," said a voice.

The Colonel nodded his agreement. Land south of the Citadel and advance on it. If the experiences of the intell teams were representative, there would be no opposition until they reached the Citadel itself. Then, if they were on the ground, there still might be no resistance at all.

"Do we know anything about the inhabitants of the planet?" asked an officer.

The Colonel reached down, used a keypad. The planet was replaced with a holo of the alien found on the asteroid. It rotated slowly, just as the planet had.

"This is the enemy, as far as we can tell," said the Colonel. "It is not very strong, isn't very clever, and is very fragile."

"Not much of an enemy."

There was a bark of laughter. The Colonel let it die out and then said, "That might be true, but it's the only enemy that we have."

CHAPTER 13

They had moved steadily through the day, stopping about noon, or what they believed to be noon, for something to eat. They had hidden in a thicket and buried the remains of the meal, though Price didn't think anyone or anything would be following them. They drank some water and then pressed on.

They crossed an open field that looked to be cultivated. The ground was soft, as if it had been plowed, but there were no straight lines of crops, just a uniformness of the plants that suggested farming. They found no buildings, no houses or equipment sheds. They discovered no roads and the one river they crossed was clean and pure. No sign of any pollution, no cans or old tires or wrecked cars. And no fish.

They continued to march, hearing nothing other than the noise they made. Nowhere could they find animals or insects or the sounds of civilization.

Then, suddenly, that all changed. Price believed they were getting close to the outskirts of the city. They had traveled ten or twelve miles and hadn't been that far from the southernmost reaches of the city.

They had been walking through a forest that had a strange, manicured look to it. Grass, or the equivalent, not a tangle of undergrowth, and trees that were evenly spaced. Clumps of bushes and trees were scattered through the forest, but even those had a regular look to them, as if someone had planned it all out carefully.

At the edge of the forest they stopped so that Price could crawl forward. There was another open field, but this had the look of a desert. It was a large area that contained almost no plants, was level, as if it had been plowed, filled with sand. Heat radiated from it, though at the upper latitudes, it wasn't as hot as it could have been if it had been located near the equator.

Right in the middle of it was a clump of machinery painted a bright red. A half-dozen creatures were scrambling over it, one of them sitting in the center of it looking as if it were the driver.

Coollege joined him, lying on her stomach beside him. She leaned close and said, "Well?"

"Looks like the little creatures from the asteroid." He handed his image enhancer to her and she lifted it to her eyes.

"Looks like it hell," she said. "It looks like a bunch of twins."

"That's what I thought too."

"Well," she said, "I guess we are on the right planet after all."

Price began to push himself to the rear. He found Monier and said, "We found someone. You getting anything?"

"No, not really. Only a feeling that the job they're doing has to be done *right now*. They're not distracted by anything else. They're focused."

"Highly disciplined," suggested Price.

"No," said Monier, shaking her head. "I don't feel it is discipline. It's something else."

Coollege asked, "What are we going to do now?"

"I'm tempted to walk out there, across the field, and see what happens," said Price.

"Not very good procedure," said Coollege.

"I don't think they'll even react," he said. "They'll just keep working away and not do a thing."

"You really going to do that?" asked Coollege.

"Not at the moment," said Price. He turned toward Monier and waited.

"I can't get anything more from them. They're completely focused on the task."

"Do you know what it is?"

She shrugged. "Has something to do with computers . . . some kind of pipeline for a cooling system . . . or rather an addition to the existing cooling system."

"How smart are they?" asked Coollege.

"I don't know . . ."

"They have equipment out there," said Price. "They're using it in coordination with one another. That implies some intelligence."

"If they built the equipment . . ."

"Jackknife," said Price, "I don't want a long discussion here and now. We've got to think of something. We can't get to the city if we don't get moving."

"So we detour around them."

"I'd like to see what they're doing out there."

"Rachel already told you," said Coollege.

Price took a deep breath and closed his eyes momentarily. "You and Monier stay here. I'll stroll out there. If I get into trouble and you can help, then do so. If not, you know what you need to do."

"Tree . . ."

"Nothing's going to happen. Besides, we need this data for the next report."

"Sure," said Coollege.

Price stripped his pack and set it on the ground. He put his rifle on top of it and then pulled his pistol. He checked it, chambered a round, then stuck it inside his shirt so that it was hidden from view.

"You know it's against the rules for you to carry that gun concealed," said Coollege, grinning.

"So arrest me."

"You're under arrest."

Price ignored that. He took a sip from his canteen and added it to the pile of gear. "If everything goes all right, bring this to me."

"Sure."

Price stood up and then without looking back walked to the

edge of the woods. He stood there for a moment and then stepped out, onto the sand. It seemed that no one saw him.

The activity on the ship was suddenly frantic. The Colonel had passed the battle orders to the subordinate commanders and wanted the various units ready to deploy in a matter of hours. Men and women were running everywhere. Gear was spilled on the decks as the soldiers sorted through it trying to determine what they would need to complete the mission and what would be nothing more than extra weight.

Over the PA system, the regimental operations officer announced, "First Battalion, Company Alpha, report to shuttle bay four in thirty minutes."

"Christ," said Susan Hyland, the company commander. "What the hell do they expect? No warning and then boom, we're to report to the shuttle bay."

Hyland was the youngest of the company commanders, having been elevated to that post on the basis of a brilliant test score and a major mistake by the old company commander who had forgotten that the position was appointed at the whim of the Colonel and not by election.

She was a stocky woman with short, dark hair, blue eyes, and a rounded face. She had a pointed chin and heavy eyebrows that nearly met over her eyes. She was well muscled and had proven to the NCOs that she was their equal in hand to hand and with any of the small arms.

"We're supposed to be ready always," said First Sergeant Robert Swain, an old man of nearly forty. His hair was salt and pepper but he was wiry and strong. No one disputed his authority. What some of the younger soldiers couldn't understand was his devotion to the company commander. Of course, he was devoted to the position not the person.

"They could have warned us. It's been a long time since they found that damned asteroid. You'd think there would have been some clue that they planned to invade. You'd think they wouldn't wait until the last minute."

"There were clues. You just missed them."

She whirled on him, glaring at him. "If you're so smart, why didn't you say something earlier?"

Swain said, "Because we're ready. All equipment has been inventoried and checked. That which needed maintenance was reported and repaired. The ammunition stocks were replaced. Laser weapons and powerpacks were checked. Stores of ready-to-eat meals, first-aid kits, medical supplies, were all inventoried. If it was damaged, expired, or spoiled, it was replaced. Vests, both ballistic and laser, were inspected. Radio gear, batteries, and scramblers have been inspected. Everything has been done, as it is on a regular basis. We're ready."

"Why wasn't I told?"

Swain grinned broadly. "All reports were logged into the mainframe. Hard copy was supplied to the company office, reviewed, and then recycled. Your initials were on each of those documents."

In her mind she could see the pile of paper that passed over her desk on a daily basis. She saw the computer screen filled with data. Coupled to the required reading, the orders that had to be issued, and the intelligence summaries, as well as correspondence that was on the electronic bulletin board and the E-mail, she knew that she must have glanced at the report, saw that it was routine, and initialed it to get it out of her box and off her desk.

"Sorry, Sergeant. I should have known."

"Captain, the running of the company on a daily basis is my job. You make the decisions on the important matters and the tactical decisions in the field. I take care of everything else."

"Of course."

"If you had spent any time as an NCO you would have known that."

"I was given no choice . . ."

Swain held up a hand. "I wasn't criticizing. I was merely commenting that those who rose through the ranks understand a little more quickly what the first sergeant does. The first sergeant and the executive officer."

Hyland couldn't help laughing. "Okay. You win. We're ready."

A lieutenant ran up and saluted. She started to speak, but Swain cut her off. "In the field, on the planet's surface, there will be no saluting."

She started to protest and then glanced at Hyland who said, "The Sergeant is right."

"Sorry." She took a deep breath and then said, quickly, "I've just lost my RTO and medic."

"What in the hell happened?"

"They were moving a crate and dropped it. RTO has four broken toes and the medic strained his back. Locked up tight so that he could barely move."

"Shit."

"If I might," said Swain. "You have an assistant RTO, or should. Just move him or her up. Third platoon has a man cross-trained as a medic. Davison, I think. Have him replace your medic."

The Lieutenant hesitated and Hyland said, "Well, what in the hell are you waiting for."

She came to attention, saluted, shot a glance at Swain, and said, "Sorry." She whirled and disappeared.

"Fifteen minutes," said the operations officer on the intercom.

"We're never going to make it," said Hyland.

"Relax, we'll make it. Besides, once we get to the shuttle bay, it'll take an hour to load both the equipment and the people. That'll give us enough slack to correct any problems we find."

Hyland felt her feet itching. She wanted to run, to shout, to do something. The energy was burning through her. Her senses seemed to be enhanced. She could see better, hear better. Her mind was racing and she felt that she could lift the shuttle and throw it to the planet.

Swain said, "I'm going to see how the first platoon is making out."

"Why?"

"Platoon sergeant took sick last week and we have a replacement in there. I want to make sure that everything is going smoothly." He noticed the look on her face and added, "I don't expect there to be a problem. I just want to make sure there isn't one."

Hyland knew that she had to do something or she would slowly go insane. There was too much activity swirling around her. "I'll be in the company office."

"Certainly, Captain. I'll bring your weapon by in about ten minutes."

Hyland cursed herself silently. She should have thought about that herself. "That's all right. I'll pick it up now, before I get to the company office."

"Five minutes," said the operations officer.

Hyland suddenly laughed. That was typical. Stand around for days and suddenly everything had to be done immediately. No time to think or plan, just do it now because it has to be done right now.

"I'll see you at the company office," said Swain.

"In a few minutes, Sergeant."

"And then we see if the training has taken."

Hyland stopped and turned back. "You know. That's sort of what frightens me."

"Me too," said Swain.

CHAPTER
~14~

Price knew that he should avoid any contact with the locals but it had taken so long to find any that he didn't want to lose the opportunity to gather a little intelligence. If they had a radio on the bulldozer, or other communications gear, then they could alert the city that aliens had landed, if those in the city didn't know it already. If those on the bulldozer even cared that aliens had landed.

He walked out of the forest like a man on a stroll through the park thinking of all the UFO reports that had been made on Earth. If they were on Earth and someone reported such an incident, no one would have believed it figuring the witness was more interested in getting his face on video or on one of the morning talk shows.

He watched the creatures as they worked. One of them looked up, stared at him for a moment, and then bent back to work. It couldn't have cared less that he was around. It held a long silver pipe while another of the creatures worked on the bottom of it. The one on the bulldozer sat there, its face turned toward the sun looking as if it were sunning itself.

When he got closer, he expected them to stop and warn him

away, but none of them seemed interested in his approach. They were standing around, working on the pipe. One grabbed a tool, banged on the pipe several times. It was the first noise that he'd heard that didn't fit the environment as a natural sound of some kind.

Price walked right up to them and stood there, looking down into the hole the creatures had dug. Two more were in the bottom of it, covered with mud. They were trying to fit two ends of pipe together.

Price stood there watching for several minutes, but the creatures ignored him. It was as if he were part of the landscape that they would have to work around.

Now that he was close to them, he could tell that these beings were like the one he'd seen on the asteroid. There was no question about it.

"Afternoon," said Price.

The creatures continued working without acknowledging him.

"What's going on here?" Price didn't expect them to understand a word he said. He hoped the sound of his voice would interest them.

But it didn't. The one on the bulldozer twisted around, started the engine, and backed up, lifting the blade, but that was the only response from any of them. It had nothing to do with Price.

"Well, I guess I'll be going." Price walked around the hole and headed off toward the north. He reached the other side of the field and moved into the trees. Once there, he turned, but the creatures hadn't stopped their work. They were still near the bulldozer and working in the hole.

A moment later Coollege approached him from inside the trees. "Well?"

"Like I wasn't there."

"So what do we do now?"

"Continue on toward the city."

"Leaving them behind us? On our lines of communication?" asked Coollege.

"I don't think they understand about lines of communication," said Price. "Further, I don't think they care about them." He looked at Monier. "Well?"

"They don't care about anything other than getting their job completed. There was no reaction from them when you approached them. Nothing at all."

"Jackknife, get that encoded and ready for transmission."

"We're not scheduled to check in again for another two hours."

"Get it ready now," said Price.

"Yes, sir."

The bedlam in the company area had been nothing compared to the confusion in the shuttle bay. The company stood in platoon formation with crates of equipment stacked around the shuttle craft. Sailors ran from one group to the next screaming orders that appeared to be contradictory. A dozen soldiers including a couple of officers were adding to the din, shouting at everyone around them. A few NCOs were running from platoon to platoon with no plan in mind. They were just moving around because they believed they had to.

Hyland stood at the hatch, pleased that her company was formed and ready to board the shuttles. They were all dressed in khaki, with body armor covering their torsos, helmets that hid everything but the eyes and nose, and weighted gloves that could be used as saps.

"Looks like a desert environment," said Hyland.

Swain, next to her, said, "Predominate color is tan. The Citadel is tan . . . desert environment clothing was required by the OPLAN."

An officer approached. She looked like a teenager. She saluted and said, "Second Lieutenant Judith Gotler."

"So?" said Hyland.

"Last-minute intell from the planet's surface."

"Can we talk here?" asked Swain.

"Why not?" asked Gotler. "No one here is going to be able to tell anyone if they hear anything they're not supposed to hear anyway."

Swain shrugged and Hyland said, "Give it to us then."

"The population, based on the reports of the ground teams, is very sparse. No large-scale cities other than the Citadel. Sensor and radar sweeps reveal nothing unusual based anywhere. There are some indications of defenses located on the closest celestial bodies. The landing will either be unopposed or there will be very light resistance."

Swain interrupted. "You're predicting that we'll either be unopposed or opposed."

"Lightly opposed."

Swain rolled his eyes. "You've told us nothing that we don't already know."

Gotler looked hurt but said, "Then what about this. One team approached a group of the enemy and they ignored him. It was as if he didn't exist. They saw him. They had to. He spoke to them, but they just kept on working."

Swain looked at Hyland. "That's going to complicate the mission."

"How?" asked Gotler, though it really was none of her business.

Hyland said, "If the locals are harmless, we can't just open fire when we see them. If they see us, do they report that to someone and if they do, does that make them a threat to us. The invading army is sometimes seen as liberators. If such is the case, we don't want to alienate the locals by indiscriminate firing. But we can't just sneak in because they have already been alerted to our presence."

Gotler shrugged as if to say she didn't really care. "You have my report," she said.

Swain looked at the troops and then at Gotler. "I think we need to have an intelligence officer to help us during the landing phase."

Hyland understood immediately. Grinning broadly, she said, "I think you're right, Sergeant. I'm authorized to take anyone or anything I need for this operation. Lieutenant Gotler, I hope you have your gear handy."

"You can't do this," she said. "Major Webb won't let it happen."

"Lieutenant," said Hyland, "I want you back here in ten minutes prepared to land with us. I'll want a complete briefing of the latest intelligence."

"No."

"You'd better hurry," said Swain.

"Major Webb will authorize it," said Hyland. "I'll talk to him."

"You can't . . ."

"You have your orders, Lieutenant, I suggest that you prepare to land with us. You certainly don't want to be seen as trying to avoid a hazardous mission. You have nine minutes."

Gotler stood as if rooted to the deck, staring from one to the other. Finally she decided that there was nothing she could do except speak to Webb in the next five minutes. Webb, as a major, could easily countermand the orders. She spun without saluting, heading to the hatch.

As it irised open, Hyland said, "You'd better get to Webb in the next two minutes and prove to him that we're going to need Gotler or we'll lose her."

"We don't need her," said Swain.

"Sure we do. Besides, seeing the result of all the information she hands out will do her some good. Get her a little seasoning as a combat officer."

Swain nodded and ran off, heading for the nearest ship's phone. He'd talk to Webb and get it straightened out.

Hyland headed across the deck, to the first platoon. Two squads had fallen out of formation and were working with the sweating sailors who were tossing the equipment pods into the shuttle. Inside, the pods were stacked on rails filled with rollers so that when the shuttle landed and the rear cargo door opened, one extremely small person could shove the whole load out onto the ground.

The platoon leader turned and said, "We'll be ready in about six minutes. We'll load the troops then and be ready for take off in eleven."

"Good."

"Will you be deploying with the first platoon?"

Hyland hadn't even thought of that. Swain would tell her which shuttle to use. It was another of the functions he fulfilled without her realizing it.

To cover, she said, "I'll let you know. I want to inspect the rest of the company."

"Yes, ma'am."

She turned and looked at the other four shuttles. The activity around them seemed to make no sense to her. A lot of people were standing in formation while others ran around throwing equipment in to the rear of shuttles.

Swain returned and said, "I just spoke to Major Webb. He was not pleased with our request, but understood the necessity of it and granted his permission. I believe, at that point, Gotler walked in and said that some infantry company was trying to shanghai her. Webb mumbled something and then Gotler exploded. She should be here in five minutes or less. She is not a happy camper."

"Good. Which shuttle are we on?"

"You'll go down with the fourth platoon. The radio gear and heavy weapons are there. They'll be setting up the headquarters with a defensive perimeter. I'll be with first. Where do you want the new lieutenant?"

"Why don't we really annoy her and send her down with the second platoon?"

"Sure, but . . ."

Hyland held up his hand. "I know. I know. You told Webb that we needed her for briefings and if we stick her off by herself, we'll catch hell when we return. But the point is that we'll need her when we land anyway."

"Whatever . . ."

Hyland then reconsidered. "She'll have to go with me."

Swain pointed to the hatch. "She made it. Even has a weapon."

A Klaxon sounded and Hyland noticed that the troops were beginning to board the shuttles. She held out a hand. "Good luck, Sergeant."

Swain took her hand and said, "See you on the planet's surface."

They worked their way through the forest. It turned out to be a thin band, no more than a mile wide. When they crossed it, they found themselves at another open field, but this time, on the horizon there were buildings. Low, one-story structures that looked as if they were made of adobe and hadn't been repaired in a long time.

With the image enhancer Price could pick up additional detail. Doors were missing from hinges and the roofs of some had collapsed. The wall of one had fallen in and there were hints of weeds overrunning parts of the built-up area. There was no sign of life.

"What do you see?" asked Coollege.

Price ignored the question and asked Monier, "Are you picking up something? Anything?"

Monier shook her head.

"Shit," said Coollege. "This isn't doing us any good at all."

Price couldn't help himself. He said, "You were concerned about her reading minds and now you don't believe her. You think that she's something of a fraud."

"I just don't want my life in the hands of someone who believes in ESP."

He stared at her for a long moment and then shook his head. "I don't want to cross that open field until dark," said Price, changing the subject.

"I'll get the radio set for the next check," said Coollege.

Monier said, "What can I do?"

"Keep watch on the city. If you see anything move, let me know. Try to find out where the enemy is located. We know there are living beings on this planet. I'd like to know where they're hiding."

"Okay."

Coollege dropped her pack and pulled the radio out. She turned it on and checked the tiny red light. Satisfied the set was working, she put the small piece of tape over it so that the light would be invisible at night.

"We need to stand by for a message," she said. "It'll be broadcast in about fifteen minutes."

"That scheduled?"

"Nope. They're putting out a message to repeat every few minutes. I'm not going to acknowledge," said Coollege.

Price looked at his watch and then up into the sky. The sun was now closer to the horizon but he didn't think it would be dark for several hours. The day seemed to last longer than that on Earth. That was something he should have learned before he'd been dropped on the planet. There were a hundred, thousand little things that should have been discovered. They were moving too fast. They were outracing their knowledge and that was the quickest way to get into trouble.

Coollege saw the thin metal tape begin to unwind itself from the interior of the radio. She read it and when the message ended, ripped it from the machine. She handed it over to Price.

"Things are beginning to move."

Price read it. "They're launching an invasion tonight? What the hell are they thinking?"

CHAPTER

15

Sergeant Wallace Stone didn't like the fact that both Price and Coollege were on the planet's surface and he was stuck on the ship. He should be there with them rather than some lieutenant that they didn't know. She wouldn't know how to handle herself on the ground, on an intelligence assignment, in combat. She was too new, too inexperienced and therefore too unpredictable.

Now Stone was being sent out in one of the small ships armed with missiles and bombs and torpedoes. He was going to help guard the invasion fleet. It was not a job he felt qualified to do, though he'd been through flight training as part of one of his assignments. It certainly wasn't the assignment that an intell NCO should have.

Sitting alone in the intell office, his feet up, with the latest intell being broadcast over the intership system, he thought about that. About the twelve months that he'd spent, as a young lieutenant commander, trying to determine if there was a spy in his class. Rumor had it that they had been infiltrated by a group from a small planet that wanted to overthrow their normal government. Because of that, Stone had gotten placed into the class as one of the three agents to locate the bad guys. Once they were identified, Stone and his friends would return to their normal assignment.

But Stone, knowing that the best way to get along in the military was to know as much of value to the military as he could, made a pact with the others. Oh, he wasn't supposed to know they were around or who they were, but he wouldn't have been a very good agent if he hadn't known. Once he was sure, he approached them and suggested that even if they learned they were infiltrated and who the bad guys were, they would keep their mouths shut until they were through with the class. Both had agreed.

The funny thing was, two days later, he learned who the bad guys were. If he hadn't been so busy trying to spot the other agents, he would have spotted them immediately. But each of the men kept his word and they continued through the school. Stone, along with the other two, graduated as pilots.

Now that training was about to put him right into the middle of the action again. He was a qualified pilot, he had seen the planet, and he had friends on the ground. That meant he would do a good job, according to the latest of the psychological studies that military planners relied upon. So he was now one of the pilots.

"All pilots please report to the shuttle bay." The message was broadcast over the ship's intercom system.

Stone let his feet drop to the desk and pulled a keyboard toward him. He put his fingers on it and typed quickly. He moved the cursor down, clicked the mouse, and shut down everything in the shop. Without the proper start-up code, no one would be able to enter any of the computers or use the terminals. That was the equivalent of locking the safe.

He stood up, took a quick look around, and then pulled a flight suit from the rack near the hatch. It had no insignia on it. Combat pilots weren't supposed to fly in suits covered with patches and insignia. That provided too much information to the enemy in the event of a crash. He fastened the Velcro and then moved to the hatch. When it irised open, he stepped out and then locked it.

He walked down the corridor wondering if it was true. It didn't appear that they were about to invade another planet. Those in the corridor were strolling along. None of them seemed to have the dedicated look of people with a mission. They didn't have the extra fast walk that suggested they had something important to accomplish. Then, he too was strolling along, but that was because he'd been around long enough to know that you didn't have to hurry to get to the place where they would make you wait.

At the shuttle bay the situation changed. There were armed guards at the hatch, but they were for show. Inside, the bedlam he expected was evident. The noise level was extreme with men and women shouting, banging on metal, trying to get the small craft ready for a coordinated launch.

"You are?" asked a sailor staring down at an electronic clipboard.

Stone didn't know exactly what to say. He had been used as a pilot as a naval officer but those orders had been rescinded when that mission had ended. If he said he was a sergeant, he was afraid that he would be replaced in the rotation. Sergeants weren't supposed to be flying as pilots. He solved the dilemma by saying, "Stone."

"Yes, sir. I have you here, Lieutenant."

Stone raised an eyebrow. Someone had thought of the problem and resolved it quickly. "Which ship?"

"Two oh six," said the sailor. He pointed to the rear of the hangar deck. "Over there, sir."

"Thank you," said Stone. He walked across the deck, reading the numbers on the craft until he found the one assigned to him. He walked around it slowly, looking for any sign of external damage that no one had repaired. Satisfied that the ship was spaceworthy, he began his preflight inspection.

When he completed that, he climbed up into the cockpit, flipped the battery switch, and checked the electrical systems, especially those related to the weapons systems. He made his commo check and inspected the sensors and radars and target acquisition system. Satisfied that his craft was completely spaceworthy, inside and out, he reported that to the control room and then sat back to wait for the orders to be issued.

Hyland sat in the darkened rear of the shuttle, waiting until it lifted off, drifted forward and out of the shuttle bay, and then unbuckled her seat belt. She leaned forward, checked on her pack, and then turned her attention to Gotler who looked as if she had just survived her first ride on the universe's largest roller coaster.

"I don't see any point in my being here," she said again.

Hyland ignored the comment and said, "Exactly what do you know about the enemy on the ground?"

Gotler rubbed her belly as if she was wondering if she was going to be sick and then said, "I told you all that I know. Everything that any of us knows."

"Why don't you tell me what you think," said Hyland evenly. "Maybe that will be more helpful."

"I don't think anything," said Gotler. "I don't know much either."

"Then I guess you must be incompetent and that's what I'll report to Major Webb when we return."

Gotler glared at her and looked as if she were going to pout. She shook herself and said, "I am not incompetent. I do not like being forced to deal with information that isn't accurate. When you begin to speculate, you begin to make mistakes."

"Trends," said Hyland. "That's what I need now. What are the trends?"

"We don't have enough information to make any sort of forecast," said Gotler.

"Shit. Tell me something."

"I don't believe there will be much of anyone on the planet. I think it is basically deserted. I think the population moved to the Citadel and then simply died out like the Mayans on Earth. They completed their task and then died because there was nothing left for them to do. They had no goal once the Citadel was finished."

"You don't think we'll meet any resistance?" asked Hyland. She had missed the comment about the enemy going the way of the Mayans.

"From an armed force? On the planet? No. I don't think there is an armed force there. I don't think there will be much of anything there."

Hyland leaned back in her seat and snorted. "We're armed to the teeth, prepared for the worst, and you don't think we'll meet any resistance."

"You asked me for my opinion," said Gotler.

"And you told Major Webb about this?"

"He was as skeptical as you are. I merely said that based on the reports it didn't appear that there was any sort of military force on the planet although there did seem to be some computer-controlled point defenses."

"Well," said Hyland, "it's an interesting theory. Of course we'll land assuming the worst."

"Of course," said Gotler.

One of the sergeants worked his way back to where Hyland was and said, "I'd like to let the troops roam a little. Let them stretch their legs. We keep them locked up in their seats and they lose the edge. They'll be useless once we make plantfall."

"Keep it reasonable. I don't want the aisles jammed. And I want the squad leaders going over the mission with them one more time."

"Yes, ma'am."

When the Sergeant turned to leave, Gotler said, "How soon do we land?"

"Invasion syllabus calls for us to be on the ground just before first light in the morning."

Stone watched on his HUD as the first of the ships slipped from the shuttle bay and disappeared into space. A second followed it and then he joined the line. The blinking rally lights on the rear of the lead ship told him which direction his flight leader had taken. Stone turned his ship, increased the power, and caught up quickly.

Stone took a wing position and once the last of the craft joined the formation, they increased their power, accelerating away from the fleet.

They made a long looping turn, flew over the fleet once, and watched as the first of the infantry shuttles began to slide into space under them. As they began to fan out, the fighter craft raced over them and took up a position in front of them. They would lead the infantry to the planet, sweeping any opposition away before the troop carriers, the slicks, could be engaged and destroyed.

They entered light speed together, but once the transition was made, Stone could no longer see the other ships through his tiny windshield. Instead, he held his position in the formation based on the HUD. The computer, sensing the locations of the other ships, showed their position on the heads-up so that Stone could avoid them.

Stone flipped on the autopilot that would maintain his position in the formation. He reached down, tugged at the straps of his seat belt and shoulder harness. It was an almost unconscious act. All throughout the flight, he would check his belts repeatedly, as if he believed they would somehow become loose.

He flew on in silence, watching the progress of the flight on the HUD. The enemy system was marked at the top, showing their progress toward it. He dozed once or twice, jerking awake after only a few minutes. He'd then check the HUD, see that they were closer to the destination, and relax.

As they approached the enemy system, Stone changed the sensor array, now searching for signs that there were enemy ships out there, but he found nothing that didn't belong. If the enemy had any ships, it was not sending them out to intercept the flight. Stone and his flight entered the enemy system unopposed. It wasn't exactly what he expected but it was certainly better than having to fight his way in.

"Blue flight, let's spread it out and decelerate to sublight. Respond in flight order."

"Two."

Stone touched a button for his radio. "Three."

"Four."

"Decelerate on my mark. Now."

Stone used the stick to send the message to the flight computer. The ship slowed rapidly and dropped into sublight speed. There was nothing to tell him that the transition had been made except for the instrumentation. Looking out the windshield now, he could see the stars had returned to normal. Space looked as it was supposed to look. And Stone could see the enemy's home star in the center of the system, glowing bigger and brighter than any of the other stars around it. They were about to invade it.

"Let's get ready people. Here we go."

Stone didn't understand why someone always had to say that regardless of the circumstances.

CHAPTER
16

When the invasion began, Price didn't know it. Neither did Coollege. They were lying in the tall grass at the edge of the city, watching, searching for lights, for movement, for any sign that the enemy was alive and well and hiding in there. But they could see nothing out of the ordinary. They saw nothing to suggest any life.

Monier was there too, but she wasn't watching the city. Her eyes were on the night sky above them, searching for any sign of the fleet. She knew it was close, not because of anything she could see, or anything that she knew, but because of what she felt.

"They're coming," she said quietly.

"Who's coming?" asked Price.

"The fleet . . . the invasion." Monier looked at Price. "They're very close now."

Coollege turned and looked at Monier. She asked, "How do you know?"

Monier pointed to the north. "They're out there about to hit the city."

Price asked, "Are you picking up anything from the locals? Anything at all?"

Monier closed her eyes and dropped her head to the ground. After a moment she said, "Nothing."

"Tree," said Coollege, "we've got to do something. Move out. Get closer. Or get the hell out of here. Especially if the invasion is going to start soon."

Price, using the image enhancer, scanned the city in front of them again. He thought that darkness would help him spot the enemy in the city. There would be lights. Electric lights or flashlights or fires or something, but the area directly in front of him was pitch-black. The only light was from the sky. One of the tiny moons and the blaze of stars.

There was no movement in that portion of the city. There had been none when they arrived. He had watched carefully, but it was obvious that the buildings were deserted. Good escape and evasive technique told him to stay away from such areas, but then, he wasn't escaping and evading and apparently no one on the planet cared that he was there.

He wanted to say that they would move out in fifteen minutes but there was no reason to delay. They'd been there for a couple of hours, they had studied the terrain carefully, and they were well fed and rested.

"Let's go," said Price. "I'll take the point. Stay ten, twelve yards behind me. Jackknife, you have the rear."

"Again."

"Again," said Price. He rolled to the right and picked up his pack. He climbed to his knees, shouldered his pack, and adjusted it. Out of habit, he checked his rifle, making sure that it was ready to fire. Without a word, he stood, moved to the very edge of the forest, and hesitated. Finally he stepped out, crouched low, and behind to jog across the open field of soft dirt. He wanted to reach the crumbling buildings as quickly as he could.

Monier followed behind him and Coollege waited until he was about halfway across the open area before she left the forest. They ran in a zigzag pattern, using the little cover available to them. Price slowed once, as if he were going to drop to the ground but didn't. He reached the buildings, ran past the first of them, and stopped at the corner of one that showed no sign of deterioration.

Monier stopped right behind him and Coollege joined them a

moment later. She was breathing hard, as if she had sprinted the last hundred yards rather than jogging. Price looked at her and raised a questioning eyebrow.

"Clear behind us," said Coollege. "Just getting a little lonesome back there. And I didn't like being out there as the only target."

"They should be starting at any time now," said Monier.

"Who?" asked Coolledge.

"The fighters," said Monier. "Our fighters. Hitting the Citadel."

"What the hell is the Citadel?" asked Price, forgetting that she had explained it to him once before.

"It's what they're calling the main part of the city now," said Monier. "They think the control of the planet is hidden in the Citadel. It's the center of power."

Price turned toward the north, staring at the dark sky overhead, searching for the strike aircraft. He thought he could see flashes of light that marked their entrance to the planet's atmosphere, but couldn't be sure.

Stone became alert when they crossed the orbit of the outermost planet of the system. He kept his eyes open, searching space outside his craft, but there was nothing for him to see. None of the instruments that radiated were turned on. Everything was in the passive mode. If the enemy was searching, using instruments like those in Stone's ship, his computer would be able to detect that. It would tell them where the enemy was because he had been foolish enough to turn on his instruments. If the enemy didn't, and Price didn't see them through his tiny window, then the two forces could pass with neither seeing the other.

But everything remained quiet. If the enemy was out there, he was as blind as Stone and his people. The HUD showed nothing other than the positions of the other fighters in the attack flight.

They continued on, flying closer to the fourth planet. They didn't use the radios, didn't use the navigation lights. They just held their position in the formation as they flew on toward the fourth planet.

Then, over shielded radio communication, Stone heard, "Let's go active."

Stone turned on the various search and acquisition radars and sensors and then studied the HUD. Nothing had changed on it. There were no enemy spacecraft around him. No enemy pickets to be seen. Just empty space except for the invasion force.

"Let's slow it up and give the slicks time to catch up," said the flight leader.

Stone watched the HUD closely, adjusting his thrusters so that he stayed in the same position relative to the flight leader.

They coasted for several minutes. The fourth planet was in the center of the HUD, a small, glowing ball. Along one side were a series of numbers giving the distance and the time to the planet based on the current speed.

When they were still more than a hundred thousand miles out, the flight leader ordered, "Let's clean it up and arm the weapons. You are cleared to fire if fired on. Do not initiate the action. They get the first shot. But they only get one."

"Two."

"Three."

"Four."

Stone laughed then. It seemed that the rules of engagement always gave the bad guys the first shot. Of course, in this situation, that kept the fighters from announcing their presence with an ill-advised shot. If the enemy took the first shot, it meant that the enemy already knew they were there.

Over the intercom, they heard, "We are about thirty minutes out."

Hyland stood up then. She had tired of sparring with Gotler. Gotler was convinced that only she knew what was going on and anyone who didn't listen to her had to be an idiot. She was too opinionated and too convinced of her own self-importance, which explained why she thought that she could talk Major Webb into saving her from having to make planetfall with an infantry company.

Hyland realized that she had made a mistake. Gotler was going to be of no value and might turn out to be a real liability. She was ill-trained to make planetfall. There was no other way to look at it.

Turning her back on Gotler, Hyland raised her voice and said,

"Squad leaders, you heard. Let's make sure we're ready to unass the craft when we touch down."

Four people, three men and one woman, stood and began working through the aisles, checking the troops and their equipment. The platoon leader was standing in the center watching as the platoon sergeant checked the equipment pods. One of the shuttle crew members was unhooking the straps, preparing to shove the gear out the instant they landed and got the cargo door open.

Hyland then bent and pulled her pack from under her seat. She opened it only so that she would have something to occupy her time. She didn't want to have to talk to Gotler anymore. She didn't even want to have to look at her.

"I'm not sure what I should have," said Gotler. "What I should have brought with me."

That seemed to be quite an admission. Hyland glanced up at her. "You went through basic training . . ."

"A year ago."

"And you've forgotten."

"Most of it."

"Well," said Hyland, "I guess you'd better concentrate on remembering." Then, feeling that was unduly harsh, and because they might be going into combat where Gotler could get killed, she said, "Let me see."

Gotler opened her pack and then stood back, away from it. "That's what we have stored in the office for emergency deployment."

"Then you haven't inspected it?"

"One of the sergeants looks at it every six months or so. That's his job."

Hyland took a deep breath and began to search through the pack carefully. Everything looked to be in good shape. None of the seals had been broken, the equipment was clean, and it was all there.

"I would have looked at it myself," said Gotler, "but you didn't give me the time."

Hyland adjusted the gear and closed the flap on the pack. She hefted it by the straps. "That should be somewhat more comfortable to wear now."

Gotler was staring at the pack. Slowly she turned her attention to Hyland. "Thanks."

Hyland stood up and watched as the rest of the platoon worked. The men and women were more interested in their weapons than the gear in the packs. In the next few hours it would be the weapons that could save them. If they lost some of the gear, it could be replaced.

The platoon leader circulated among the troops, randomly inspecting the packs and weapons and asking quiet questions. Satisfied that everything was ready, she turned and walked over to Hyland.

"I think we're ready for the landing."

"I want the first squad out to secure the area around the shuttle. They are to deploy with nothing else to do until the shuttle is gone again. Then integrate them back into the operation."

"Yes, ma'am."

Hyland looked at her watch, surprised that nearly twenty minutes were gone. They were getting close. Then, almost as if to confirm what she had noticed, the intercom came on. "Ten minutes to touchdown. We are in the planet's atmosphere."

The level of activity increased. The troops were lining up facing the exits in squad order. They were standing in the aisles, weapons at the ready, helmets on, the chin straps buckled, and the visors down. Almost every square inch of skin was covered to prevent insect bite, sunburn, and laser weapon wounds.

"We'll go out after the second squad and before the third," said Hyland.

"Of course."

Hyland looked back at the soldiers in the shuttle. There was no question that they were ready. They were tense, standing there unable to see outside the shuttle. There was nothing for them to do but wait.

Over the intercom, the pilot announced, "The fighters are beginning to engage the Citadel. We are in the clear. No one seems interested in us."

"Good," said Gotler.

Hyland looked at the younger woman and then realized that she wasn't that much younger. Maybe a year or maybe just a couple of months. Age in the military was not related to how

long you have been alive but on how long you had been in
the service and what you had done. In other arenas the men
and women on the shuttle would be considered boys and girls.
Most of them were barely out of high school and their teens.
Some of them hadn't reached their twentieth birthday yet. But
in the military many of them were considered experienced old
hands.

"Five minutes," said the pilot.

Hyland waited patiently, trying to keep her mind focused on
the job at hand. What she would do the moment she set foot
on the planet's surface. What she would do if the enemy fired
at her, if they attacked, if they attacked in mass. Or what she
would do if there was no reception.

"You scared?" asked Gotler.

Hyland thought about that and realized that she wasn't scared.
She was going to be too busy to be scared. She had too much to
do . . . besides, she was too well trained to be scared.

But to Gotler she said, "Everybody's scared."

"Good."

Hyland let her fingers work their way along the side of her
weapon, checking it again.

"Prepare to land," said the pilot.

Hyland yelled, "Let's get ready. No one fucks up. We do this
by the book."

A second later she felt a slight bump as the shuttle touched
down and the rear door sprang open. She didn't need to issue
another order. The soldiers were getting out rapidly. Leaping
from the rear of the shuttle.

And then she was out, on an alien planet, wondering just what
the hell she was doing there.

CHAPTER 17

"Let's stay out of the way of their weapons," said the flight leader. "Draw their attention, but don't get hit. I'm rolling in."

Stone, holding back, just outside the planetary atmosphere, waited. On the HUD, he watched as the first of the fighters from another squadron made their run. His flight leader was right behind the last of those craft as if he was following them in.

The fighter dove through the clouds but that made no difference to Stone. He could watch with his sensors on. The ship dropped to twelve thousand feet, flew straight and level for ten seconds, and then began to spin.

If there was anyone awake in the Citadel, they didn't notice the beginning of the attack. The second ship followed, twisting and turning, trying to avoid the path taken by his leader. He dropped lower, to about eleven thousand, but still there was no response.

The rest of that flight made their runs, dodging around the sky as if they expected to be taken under fire at any moment. When the flight finished the first run, they climbed as a unit, heading out of the atmosphere. They didn't have a chance to engage the enemy.

Now it was the turn of Stone's flight. They were diving

through the atmosphere at a steep angle. The nose of his ship began to heat and glow a dull cherry, but they didn't shallow the dive as was standard operating procedure. They continued on, stringing out so that only one ship would be over the Citadel at a time. They didn't pull out at eleven or twelve thousand feet, but kept on, down to eight thousand. As they punched through the lower cloud deck, the first of the beam weapons opened fire. A short burst that stabbed out and touched the nose of the lead ship.

"That's got it," said the flight leader. "We are now cleared to fire."

The flight climbed upward and then turned one hundred eighty degrees before diving back at the Citadel. The flight leader punched off several missiles. As they flashed into the night, the flight leader turned again, diving toward the ground and attempting to get away.

Beams flashed from the Citadel, reaching out toward the missiles. One by one they flared brightly and disappeared in fireworks displays.

The second ship jinked right and left, fired his missiles, and pulled away in a steep climb. The missiles were destroyed almost as they came off the rails. Then the beam reached out again, touched the rear of the ship, and cut it off. The nose tumbled upward and then began a long arcing descent. Again the beam flashed, hitting the nose section, engulfing it, and then destroying it.

Stone, who watched on the HUD, broke off his attack, diving down and away. He made a long looping turn, and then attacked. He fired two missiles and then dropped down again, trying to use part of the city for protection, staying away from the Citadel and its weapons.

The missiles, corkscrewing in, tried to avoid the beams that flashed in defense. They missed first, disappeared, and then fired again. Both missiles flew into the beams and vanished in bursts of light.

But the beams didn't target Stone. He was too far from them and too low. Instead they anticipated the next ship. As it turned toward the Citadel, a single beam stabbed out, hit the front of the ship, and then followed it. The ship twisted right and left, but the beam stayed with it. The pilot salvoed his missiles, trying to draw the beam away from his but that didn't work. Other beams reached out and destroyed the missiles.

Four dropped down, trying to get away from the beam. He hit the top of a building, bounced upward and into one of the beams. It sliced through the ship, almost cutting it in half. An instant later it exploded into a ball of fire and flame, the debris raining back to the Citadel.

"You've lost Four," said Stone.

"Roger that. Form on me."

"Say instructions."

"We're getting the hell out of here."

"Roger that," said Stone. He spotted the leader in front of him, about ten thousand feet higher than he was. He accelerated, climbing out, hoping he was out of range of the Citadel's weapons.

Behind him the next flight rolled in, but they came in together, spread out, all firing at once. The Citadel opened up, the beams sprouting from it like the grass on a field. Red and yellow beams flashed, striking out at the missiles.

"Let's break off," said the flight leader.

As one, the four ships of the flight turned, one diving, one climbing, and one each turning right or left. They were doing everything they could to confuse the targeting system in the Citadel.

Every missile fired was targeted and hit. All disappeared in blossoming explosions of yellow-orange, only one getting closer than a klick. When the missiles were eliminated, the beams faded from sight.

"All fighters egress. All fighters egress."

"None too soon," said Stone.

"All fighters join on lead flight."

Stone didn't know where the lead flight was, but it didn't matter at the moment. He just continued to climb, higher into the atmosphere, away from the enemy.

"Have we completed the mission?"

There was a hesitation and then a voice said, "Knock off the idle chatter."

"Yeah," said Stone. They weren't going to broadcast an answer to that question. The enemy, whoever it might be, could be monitoring the frequency and there was no sense in giving him the answer. Of course, the odds of that were long, given the situation, that the enemy would be monitoring their combat frequencies, but there was no reason to take the chance.

On the HUD, Stone noticed the four blips that marked the location of the lead flight. It was obvious that they were getting out.

None too soon, thought Stone, again.

There was a single, deafening roar, a flash of bright light, and the shuttle was gone. As it disappeared into the night sky, the noise of the engine fading, Hyland realized just how alone they were. Around the planet there were other companies landing, but the line was stretched thin and the communications had yet to be established.

Swain appeared, as if by magic, but didn't salute. "Company is down and deployed. All equipment made it intact."

"That's something," said Hyland. "Are we ready to move out now?"

"Everything is set, Captain."

Hyland took a moment to look around. They were on an open area between two sections of buildings. It looked like the greenbelts that were being designed into cities on Earth. The only difference was that there was nothing green growing around them.

Although the buildings were more than a hundred or more yards away and it was night, it appeared they had been abandoned. No sign of light and no sign of life.

Swain seemed to read Hyland's mind. "I got patrols out already to make sure there's no ambush hiding in there." He turned to face the closest buildings, but didn't point. Too many people in too many wars have been killed by snipers because they were pointing and therefore appeared to be officers. Or if not officers, important.

"Looks to be abandoned."

Swain didn't answer that. "I think it'll take us about four hours to get to the rally point if I read the maps right and the distances."

"Who do you want on the point?" asked Hyland.

Swain looked at Gotler standing to one side looking as if she were about ready to bolt. Her rifle was clutched in both hands. Her knuckles were white.

"How about Lieutenant Gotler?"

Hyland failed to hide her grin but said, "No. She'll be with me. Give the point to the first platoon. I want to get moving quickly."

"Yes, ma'am."

As Swain disappeared, giving the orders to the various platoon leaders and sergeants, Hyland said, "The best place to gather intelligence is on the point."

"I don't gather, I interpret. There is a difference." She stood quietly for a moment and then asked, "Do you think there will be contact?"

"Doesn't look like it," said Hyland. "Doesn't look like there is anyone around."

"Good."

The troops fanned out with those from the first platoon taking a position closest to the buildings. When the gear was distributed and the soldiers were ready, first platoon moved out slowly, spreading across the open area until they covered nearly half a klick. They were taking no chances by bunching up.

When they were nearing the first group of buildings, the second platoon started off. The whole company began to move finally, spread over the open field.

They entered the built-up area but there was no sign of life. Sand had drifted against some of the buildings. Doors hung open and windows were broken. No light showed anywhere. The soldiers were forced to use image enhancers to see anything at all. They began to break open doors so that they could search the interiors.

Hyland, taking her turn in the rotation, kicked one door open and dove through. But the interior was empty except for a broken chair thrown into a corner. She picked it up and saw that one of the legs was missing. It was a small chair, looking as if it belonged to a child.

All the windows were broken and dirt was spread across the floor, piling up against the interior wall. It was obvious that no one had crossed it recently.

Keeping her back against the rough stone wall, she moved to

the short staircase. She could see into the upper hall. There was nothing up there either. Apparently everything of value had been carried off long ago.

Once outside, she watched as the company cleared the street, finding nothing of use. They worked their way down the long street without learning a thing about the creatures who had built and lived in the city and then abandoned it.

Swain finally broke away and ran over to where Hyland stood near an intersection. There were no street signs or streetlights or even any trash. Just the sand that was invading and threatening to cover everything over.

"I'm thinking of the Mayan cities on Earth. Abandoned for no apparent reason, reclaimed by the jungle . . . only here, it's the sand."

"You're getting philosophical, Sergeant," said Hyland.

"Nope. Just thinking of what it would have been like if we'd found one of the Mayan cities fifty years after it had been abandoned. That's all."

"I think we can assume that there are no enemy soldiers hidden in this section of the city. We have seen nothing, taken no fire, and found no evidence of any armed force. Let's head on to the rally point."

"I must say, Captain, that a well-hidden enemy could be sitting around here somewhere."

"If it was on our lines of communication, I would agree, but we're not coming back here. If and when we are extracted, we'll extract from our location. We will not be required to return here or to the field we used for landing."

"Shall I alert the first platoon?"

"Let's take a ten-minute break. Full security out, but everyone gets a chance to take a drink of water, eat a candy bar, or whatever."

"By whatever do you mean take a piss?"

"And leave evidence of our passing?" asked Hyland.

"You mean like our footprints in the sand and the kicked-in doors along the street."

"Exactly."

"I'll get on it right now," said Swain.

• • •

"According to my calculations," said Price, "we should be getting close to one of the landing teams."

"Lieutenant?" asked Coollege.

Monier, who was crouched next to a large rock, said, "I know what you're thinking." And then she realized that she shouldn't have said that. "I mean, you think that I should be able to pick up on the soldiers."

"Exactly."

Price said, "I'm getting a little tired of the bickering here. It will end now."

"Yes, sir," said Monier.

"Sorry, Tree."

"Now, if you two are through, has either of you noticed anything?"

"You mean that the sand has been disturbed around here, looking as if a large force has been through?" asked Coollege.

"Exactly," said Price. "I'm glad to see that you're still paying attention."

"But we don't know whose force it is," said Coollege.

"Rachel?"

"Human. Definitely human."

"Now how can she tell that?"

Price said, "It doesn't really matter because she is right about it."

Coollege looked at him. "How do you know?"

Price held up a knife still in the scabbard. The clasp that held it to the pistol belt was broken. Someone had dropped it but didn't know it.

"Okay," said Coollege. "Where are they?"

Without thinking, Monier pointed. "In that direction. Not far from us. Want me to take the point?"

"No," said Price. "They don't know we're back here so they might be a little trigger-happy."

"Oh, good," said Coollege. "Why wasn't that arranged before we left."

Price shot her a glance and wondered what her problem was. The answer to her question was clear. The invasion started early. Price had expected to be off the planet's surface long before the first of the infantry landed.

"How do we do this?" asked Monier.

"Very carefully," said Price. "I'll take the point. We move quietly and carefully."

"I'll watch the rear," said Coollege.

They moved off then, crossing the rest of the open area and into the city itself. They moved along the street, watching for signs of anyone anywhere. They crossed the street, rounded a corner, and kept on going, searching.

It took them thirty minutes to find the rear guard of the infantry. When that happened, letting them know they were being followed was easier than Price had thought it would be. One of the soldiers of the rear guard spotted him, stepped into the street, and aimed a rifle at him. Price raised his hands above his head and yelled, "I'm Captain Price. Take me to the company commander."

"Come forward and be recognized, Price."

Price walked forward slowly and watched the barrel of the soldier's rifle. When it dropped away from his chest, he said, "I assume I'm recognized."

"Yes, sir. Come with me."

"I have two others with me."

"Let's all go." He turned and started off.

It was as easy as that.

CHAPTER
18

The Colonel looked at the assembled pilots and said, "You're going to have to do it again."

"Again?" said Stone quietly, but not quietly enough.

The Colonel looked at him and said, "I'm afraid so. We want a diversion as the seven companies that have been landed advance on the Citadel."

"Diversion?" said one of the others.

"Is there an echo in here?" The Colonel glanced at the woman who had just spoken. "Sometimes," he said, "we're required to sacrifice for the greater good."

"Bullshit!"

The Colonel turned his gaze on Stone but Stone was not intimidated.

"Let me see if I can clarify that then," said the Colonel evenly. "In this case the diversion will serve an important purpose."

"Yes, sir," said Stone.

"The plan," said the Colonel, "is to keep the enemy in the Citadel so busy worrying about the air threat that they will pay no attention to the advancing ground forces. By the time they perceive this as a threat, the infantry will be in the shadow of the walls."

"Colonel," said Stone, raising his hand slightly, "why is this necessary?"

"Are you questioning the orders?" The Colonel's voice was turning nasty.

"No, sir. I was just wondering the motive for this particular mission. They have not ventured from their system in strength. Hell, it doesn't seem they have ventured out at all except for the asteroid and a few pickets scattered around close to home."

"I would have thought that the answers would be self-evident," said the Colonel. "Every time we have come into contact with them, it has cost lives of our people. Several of those who landed on the asteroid died. They have fired on us first each time we have encountered them."

"Yes, sir," said Stone. He decided that it was now time to keep his mouth shut. Nothing he said was going to change any minds on the regimental staff. The die was long cast and it seemed that the staff believed that the enemy was hostile toward them.

"We will begin our mission, with all available craft, fully loaded, at 0600. It will be designed as a mission to destroy the Citadel. Now, I don't believe that we will be successful in that attack, but I want the mission designed that way."

He looked at the assembled pilots. "We're going to destroy that Citadel and stop the threat from this planet. Once they understand that we have the capability to do that, I'm sure that communications can be opened between our people and the enemy in the Citadel."

"We have tried communication?" asked one of the officers who rarely spoke at such meetings. He preferred to sit quietly in the back and listen.

"Ever since we made contact with the asteroid, we have attempted communication in many different ways. We have been met with hostile attitudes. There is nothing else we can do."

"What happens if we destroy the Citadel?"

"Then our problems are solved before the infantry assault," said the Colonel. "With the Citadel out of operation, we will own that planet. We can then establish communications with the inhabitants without having to worry about them shooting at us."

Stone wasn't sure if that was right or not. He did know

that everything did seem to be concentrated in the Citadel and that the enemy seemed to be extremely hostile. If the Citadel was eliminated, then there would be no organized opposition anywhere else.

"There is a lot to be done before the attack," said the Colonel. "If there are no other important questions, I suggest we all get back to work."

The men and women in the briefing room came to attention as the Colonel walked to the hatch. As soon as he was gone, the room exploded into a hundred conversations.

Stone looked around and shook his head. It didn't seem that anything in this campaign had been well thought out. But then, it wasn't up to him to decide that. He was not required to approve of the tactics or the overall plan. It was his job to follow his orders.

At 2130 hours, Hyland walked over to the jump-off point, an arbitrary location chosen only because it was in an open area that was shielded from the Citadel by a pattern in the lava. Monier, dressed in black as she had been when she landed on the planet's surface, was sitting on the ground, her back against a short wall built from black lava, and eating from a dark green can.

"When we move out," said Hyland, "I want you near me at all times. I want to know the instant you begin to receive any impressions from the Citadel. Anything at all."

Monier looked up, the plastic spoon halfway between the can and her mouth. She was surprised by the comment. "Then you don't question my ability."

"Since you're here and Captain Price assures me that he has confidence in your ability, I have confidence in your ability. I want you close to me."

Monier dropped her spoon into the can. "You sure this is a good idea?"

Hyland misunderstood the question and said, "It's a lousy idea. It stinks. But there is nothing we can do about it except try to stack the deck so that we survive. We reach the damned wall, look around, and then sneak away into the night. The only thing that I can think of is for us to look as nonhostile as possible and hope the Citadel ignores us. If we are not a threat to it, it might leave us alone. That is the only thing that I can think of."

"It doesn't sound like any of this is well thought out," said Monier.

"I suppose," said Hyland, "that from one point of view, it's not. But the brass are looking for a way to crack the Citadel and until we do it, they'll keep coming up with wild-ass plans like this one."

"Has anyone really thought about how the Citadel is going to react?"

Hyland shook her head. "We just don't know enough about it to make any assumptions."

Swain appeared. His uniform was sweat-stained although it wasn't that hot, yet. He slipped to one knee to rest. "Captain, battle lines are to be drawn in about ten minutes."

"Officers' call in three."

"Yes, ma'am."

"You stay close to me, Monier," Hyland repeated.

"I'll need to talk to Captain Price."

"You go right ahead, but I want you here before we jump off."

As Monier walked away, the platoon leaders and the executive officers began to arrive. Hyland thought about the coded orders that she had received only a few minutes earlier. It didn't seem logical to attack the Citadel without some kind of preliminary reconnaissance, but no one had asked her opinion. They had just sent down the orders and now she had to figure out the best way to execute them.

She waited as the officers crowded close. "In the next few minutes," she said, "we begin the ground assault." She waited for a response but when there was none, said, "We will, of course, use standard fire and maneuver tactics, but no one is to fire until we are shot at by the defenders of the Citadel. If we approach slowly and carefully we might not be viewed as a threat."

She continued on for the next several minutes, explaining what she thought were the best methods, what the line order of the platoons would be, and what weapons would be used. She sketched it out quickly and then looked at the assembled officers.

"Sounds like a pretty flimsy plan to me," said Stephen Cross, the second platoon leader. Like all the other junior officers, he was young and eager, and searching for great glory.

Hyland pivoted so that she could stare at Cross. He was one of the few officers who hadn't seen combat, so nerves were expected and nerves made him talk. Hyland asked, "Are there any other relevant comments?"

There were none.

"All right," said Hyland, "everyone rejoin your units and be ready in"—she glanced at her wrist, shielding the LCD on her watch from the bright sun—"two minutes and fifteen seconds."

Price and Coollege stood at the rear of the formation and listened to the pep talk given by Hyland. Price thought about the last few hours spent with the infantry. They had watched as Hyland ran her company as they all had slipped into the position among the buildings about twelve thousand yards away from the Citadel. They had spent the night watching and listening to everything around them.

When the briefing was over, Coollege leaned close to him and whispered, "I have to agree with that young officer. I don't think this is very well thought out."

Price nodded and took a deep breath. "There is something going on here. The Colonel, or someone on high, believes that we must take care of this now. That Citadel must be leveled for some reason."

"To prove to the locals that we are powerful?" suggested Coollege.

"I don't know. Every time we have encountered these people, we have been able to defeat them. First their asteroid traps us, but we get out of it . . . defeat it if you think it through. Then our scouts encounter their pickets and blow through them without much trouble. One scout orbits their home planet and gets out." Price wasn't aware of the results of the attack by the fighters the night before. That information had not been shared with the forces on the ground.

"So there is no reason to reduce the Citadel by storm," said Coollege.

"None that I can think of. This is just some kind of macho play by the brass . . ." He fell silent for a moment and then changed tactics. "If this was Earth, we'd have everything we have out to defend ourselves. Nothing would get close to our home world."

"But here we are, on the planet's surface. We landed a large force and there is no resistance."

"That's what doesn't make sense," said Price. "Here we are threatening their world but they don't seem to care."

Coollege felt her stomach turn over. Suddenly she was cold. "They only defend the Citadel," she said. "It is the only place on the planet's surface that we have seen any sort of activity that makes sense." She hadn't forgotten the creatures and the pipeline, but they had made no sense to her.

"Which means that the infantry is going to get chopped all to hell as they approach it," said Price. He was suddenly sure of that analysis.

"We going to tell Hyland?"

Price didn't answer her. He turned and started walking toward Hyland. Coollege followed behind him. All around the soldiers were getting ready for the assault. They would leave the packs behind, taking only their water, first-aid kits, weapons, and ammo. Nothing else would be needed.

"Captain," called Price as he approached, "can I talk to you for a moment?"

Hyland stopped and looked back at him. "I've got a lot to do."

"Captain," said Price, "I was dropped on this planet before you to evaluate the situation. Then, not waiting for that evaluation, the Colonel landed part of his regiment here."

"I am aware of that."

"The point," said Price, "is that the only place on this planet the enemy has attempted to defend is the Citadel. The only place on this planet that seems to have a function is the Citadel. They have made no real effort to stop us anywhere else."

"And we have made no real push to take it," said Hyland. "That's what we're about to do."

"Might I suggest, that if you are still in communications with the battalion commander, a delay in the schedule."

For the first time, it looked as if she was worried. "What do you have?"

Price glanced back at Coollege and then said, "Nothing firm, but then, our job is to take our observations and those of the soldiers around us and translate them into meaningful information."

"So . . . and remember the clock is running."

"It seems to me . . . us," said Price, hitchhiking a thumb at Coollege, "that they will defend the Citadel with everything they have. We're all walking into a trap of sorts."

"Based on your analysis of the situation," said Hyland.

"Exactly," said Price.

"Then might I suggest you communicate that to the battalion commander yourself and leave me to prepare for the upcoming assault."

"But . . ."

Hyland cut him off. "But nothing. I have a great deal of work to do before the assault begins and I have about thirty seconds to get it done." She hurried off, suddenly running toward one of the sergeants.

"Now what?" asked Coollege.

"First we let battalion know and then we stick with them to watch the show. Someone has to be available to explain what happened here."

"Great," said Coollege. "Can't we just review the combat holos and speculate from there."

"Maybe there is something we can do . . ." Price stopped talking as the infantry formed their lines to begin the assault, " . . . but I doubt it."

"Where's Monier?"

"I told her to help Hyland. Maybe she'll pick up something that'll stop the slaughter."

"But you don't think so," said Coollege.

"Unfortunately, no."

CHAPTER

19

The seven companies of the provisional assault battalion were now prepared to move on the Citadel. Hyland cocked her head to the right, as if it would help her hear the direct radio link to the other companies. The orders for the assault would be coordinated by the radio.

For a moment Hyland's company stood in the bright sunlight staring at the buildings in front of them. Over the tops they could see the Citadel, an imposing structure that dominated that area like a cathedral in a European city on the Earth.

When Hyland finally heard the coded sequence, she lifted one hand over her head and then dropped it. The first elements of the company moved forward, disappearing among the buildings. They were followed by the second wave, moving forward slowly as those in front covered the advance. As they fell into firing positions using the available cover, the last group was up and moving. Hyland, Price, and Coollege were with them, running across the sand and outcroppings of lava until they reached the shelter of the buildings about a hundred yards in front of them.

They worked their way through the town one street at a time, but they didn't worry about clearing the buildings. Now they were sure that the city was deserted. They made sure that there

were no enemy soldiers falling in behind them to cut off their
line of retreat, and then advanced until they reached the edge
of the last ring of buildings. The only thing now between them
and the Citadel was an expanse of black lava rock and fingers
of tan-colored sand.

They crossed an imaginary demarcation line and the air above
them was split with the roar of aircraft engines. The drones,
launched earlier by fighters from the fleet, dropped out of the
cloudless sky, heading straight for the Citadel. The air defense
system opened fire, at first throwing up a solid sheet of laser
beams, as if they were shooting just to be shooting.

Far overhead the fighters began a bombing run, releasing their
armaments at eighty thousand feet. The bombs, all guided, fell in
a series of formations that would drop into a pattern that should
open holes in the Citadel walls for the advancing troops.

Almost at the instant that the bombs began to fall, the main
fleet fired a salvo of missiles that would add to the confusion in
the air over the Citadel.

That was the plan developed over the last thirty hours by the
Colonel in consultation with the officers of the fleet.

Ignoring the soldiers, the defenses along the top of the Citadel began to independently target the various weapons falling
on it, blasting the closest bombs first. There were dozens of
aerial explosions, the debris flaring brightly creating patterns
of smoking trails against the deep blue of the alien sky. The
conclusions of the explosions sounded like someone pounding
on a bass drum somewhere in the distance.

The drones all vanished at nearly the same instant as the
particle beams stabbed out, touching them. With that problem
eliminated, the Citadel began searching the sky for the fighters
that had dropped the bombs. Most of them had climbed higher,
out of effective range and the beams dancing around to keep them
that way.

When the bombs had all been destroyed, the laser cannon
of the Citadel switched to the missiles that were corkscrewing
through the upper atmosphere, trying to outguess the attacker's
offensive computers. At the extreme range, there may have been
some hits, but the beams were too weak to punch through the
protective covers of the missiles. They continued on, weaving a

pattern of pure white condensation trails behind them.

The only thing the early evasive maneuvers did was teach the enemy the system being used. When the missiles finally got into the range, the laser cannon opened fire in a predetermined sequence that splattered one missile after another. Some of the remains of the weapons fell on the Citadel, but the pieces were so small that they did no damage. The larger pieces of the missiles had been independently targeted and hit again by the laser cannons. The enemy was taking no chances during this attack.

Of the three waves of the aerial assault, the bombs had gotten the closest, only because they were falling. With the other threats eliminated, the enemy point defense system began to target the bombs, destroying the last about three thousand yards above it, and then destroying the shrapnel that the explosion had produced.

Hyland, unaware that the air assault had been a dismal failure, was actually feeling good. She had heard the explosions near the top of the Citadel. She had seen the bursts of light and the clouds of smoke created by them. She didn't believe the enemy could withstand a coordinated aerial assault.

The company was now only about six thousand yards from the Citadel's walls and not a single shot had been directed at her or her company. She was concerned that there had been no explosions anywhere on the Citadel proper, but then she knew that she couldn't see everything that was happening. She dropped down into a depression in the lava and waited for the people behind her to pass by her.

Spread out in front of her, lying in the holes in the lava beds, behind the large lava boulders, or behind the debris that had been created as the Citadel had been constructed, Hyland could see about a third of her company. It was difficult to pick some of them out because the camouflage of the uniforms they wore and the blinding light from the sun overhead made it almost impossible to see anything without the helmet filters. She was sure that the defenders in the Citadel were having an equally difficult time.

Hyland crawled across a stretch of sun-hot lava, scraping her hands and knees on the sharp surfaces. She didn't know why she suddenly felt the urge to stay down, but knew that it seemed like the thing to do.

She approached Monier who was kneeling behind a large black rock, peeking over the top of it. Hyland asked, "You getting anything from inside the Citadel? We do any damage to them?"

"No. I'm not reading anything from the interior. I don't understand it. I should be able to read something."

Hyland watched as the last third of the company leapfrogged into the lead position, spreading out and then taking cover behind the rocks and debris. "Here we go again," said Hyland.

Together they got to their feet and sprinted across the hard surface of the lava, keeping as low as possible. Hyland could feel the stone flaying at the soft rubber of her boots. They ran between the people who had been on the front line, and then fanned out, searching for places to hide.

Monier rolled to her back in a deep depression that was filled with soft but hot sand. Without waiting for the question, she told Hyland, "Still nothing. They must be well shielded in there."

Hyland stood up to motion the next wave forward, but they were already up and running, dodging across the broken surface of the lava bed. They seemed to loom out of the shimmering heat as if they were ghosts from a phantom army.

As they ran by her, Hyland twisted around to watch them weave and shift as they searched for cover. In the instant before they were to drop from sight the Citadel came to life. Laser cannons that had been aimed upward to deal with the aerial threat swiveled around and lowered the barrels so that they could fire. The beams shot out, touched the advancing soldiers briefly in a crisscrossing pattern that left no one an escape, and then vanished completely. In less than a second, a third of the attacking force was dead on the lava.

Hyland came up to her knees, forgetting about the need for cover. She stared at the bodies. Smoke curled upward from the clothing, skin, and hair. Not one of them moved, or tried to get off that lava. There was a single quiet moan as one of the soldiers, apparently only wounded, tried to roll to his stomach and then stand. A single bright beam stabbed out and the soldier collapsed, dead. It was the only motion she saw after the Citadel had fired.

From the right, one trooper leapt from his cover and ran toward a fallen friend. As the trooper crouched, to grab the wounded soldier, another single beam fired and the trooper dropped to the lava in such a way that it was clear that he had been killed. No one else, nothing else, moved.

"All companies withdraw," crackled the radio. "All companies withdraw."

Hyland hesitated, unsure what to do. She glanced at Monier. "Anything?"

"Nothing. Maybe it's heavily shielded. Or maybe their minds are so different that I don't understand what I'm getting. I don't know."

Swain, using the little cover available, crawled toward Hyland. He dropped to the lava next to her. "We have been ordered to withdraw."

"I heard the order, Sergeant."

"Yes, ma'am."

Hyland was staring at the long line of scattered bodies that ringed the Citadel. She turned and sat down, her back against the rough stone of a lava boulder, eyes fixed on the ground. There was something that Monier had said that had raised a red flag but she didn't have time to worry about it now. She had other problems facing her.

"Captain?" said Swain.

Far off to her left she could see the company there on their feet fleeing. It was an orderly withdrawal. They had learned the advantage of getting out of anything they had gotten themselves into long ago. Unplanned flight did nothing but expose the survivors to the danger.

Hyland stood without a word, running to the rear. She didn't bother to look back because she knew that the rest of the company would follow her lead. And she knew that the Citadel wouldn't fire at them now. They were not moving toward it, but away from it.

She didn't stop until she reached the company area. Then she dropped to the lava and wiped the sweat from her face. She watched the remainder of the company straggle in and sit down around her. There was no talking among them. They were too stunned, too shaken, to talk. It was the first time that many of them had gone into battle. They hadn't fired a shot and lost about a third of their number. Everyone had friends lying under the hot sun, the fluids baking from their bodies. They just didn't want to talk about it.

Price stood under the canvas cover that had been erected next to a giant outcropping of lava to create a little shade. He stood with a hand on the lava and watched as the soldiers staggered in. It was an army that had been beaten. One that had been slaughtered in a few moments of battle. He could see the look of defeat on their faces and knew that if there was a way to get off the planet, they would take it without question. At the moment, they didn't want to go back into battle. They wanted to get the hell out.

Coollege was sitting with her back to them. She didn't want to watch. "We should have known."

"Known what?" asked Price.

"That would happen . . ." She hitchhiked a thumb over her shoulder.

Price stared down at her. "I told Hyland . . . I tried to advise the battalion to be careful."

"We should have been more forceful," said Coollege. "We should have told them that the enemy would fire at them with the laser weapons."

Price was about to respond and then thought better of it. She did have a point. They should have suspected that the Citadel would turn the weapons on the soldiers as the aerial assault was eliminated.

Hyland appeared then, looking haggard and tired. She sat down without a word, picked up a loose piece of lava, and examined it as if she had never seen anything so fascinating. Finally she said, "We got hammered. We didn't even get close."

Price nodded and said, "It did seem to deal with the threats on a sliding scale . . ." He rubbed his chin slowly. "It took out the most damaging assault first."

"We did get closer than the other units," said Hyland, almost as if trying to alibi the poor showing.

"What did Monier say?" asked Coollege.

"Nothing," said Hyland. "She didn't have a clue."

Price sat down beside her. "It wasn't your fault."

"No," said Hyland, "I don't need this. I know that it wasn't my fault. But I have friends out there. Lots of good people are dead . . ."

"I don't think that a frontal assault is a good idea ever," said Price.

"Now you mention it," said Hyland. Her voice was dull, tired, lifeless.

"There has got to be a way to crack that thing," said Coollege.

"If that little creature were still alive," said Price, "we could ask it a few questions. Maybe it could provide us with a clue."

"What are you talking about?" asked Hyland.

Price waved a hand. It would do no good to tell her that they had a valuable intelligence source that had died before they could exploit it. Maybe they would have had a better picture of the Citadel if the creature had been able to tell them about it before they arrived here . . . if they had known enough to ask the right questions of it at the time.

"So now what do we do?" asked Coollege.

"Our jobs. We get with the people, debrief them, and see if they saw something that we didn't. Maybe there was something that we can exploit."

"I wish you'd wait," said Hyland. "This has been quite a shock."

"I know," said Price, "but it's fresh in the mind. The details are beginning to fade already. It's the details that we have to get."

One of the sergeants, in sweat-stained and dirty khakis, appeared. "Special signal from the fleet. They want an acknowledgment in ten minutes."

Hyland slammed a fist onto her thigh and said, "Why can't they give us a chance to sort through it. Just a few fucking minutes to ourselves."

"Maybe they've figured it out," said Price.

"Right," said Hyland. "And it will cost the lives of more of my people."

CHAPTER 20

Hyland took the coded message and read it quickly. Then slowly she wadded it into a tiny ball of paper but didn't throw it away. That wasn't sound military procedure. She stared at the paper and shook her head.

The orders were simple. The Colonel and his staff had decided that a blatant frontal assault, no matter how complex and coordinated, would eventually fail. The enemy would see it coming and repeal it, and they couldn't put together a force of sufficient size to overwhelm the Citadel's defenses. A series of small raids, however, designed to breach the walls might succeed. Even if they failed, the information gathered might allow them to find a weakness to exploit by another, larger assault force. Without the pyrotechnic of a high-altitude bombing and missile attack, or a large-scale assault, the small units might be overlooked.

Price was standing right behind her. She glanced over her shoulder, indicated the orders. She asked, "You see it?"

"Yeah."

"It won't work," she said. "More fodder for the cannon."

Price, standing there on the rough broken lava of some extinct volcano and sweating in the afternoon sun, shook his head. He

151

wasn't sure that Hyland wasn't right. It was a suicide mission designed to test the defenses with the lives of the soldiers on the planet's surface. Those on the ships of the fleet didn't understand the situation on the ground. That meant that Price was failing at his job.

"I'm not going to do it," said Hyland evenly. "I can't do it."

Price said, "There might be something I can do if I can get some information to the Colonel."

"You can use every aspect of the communications facilities here," said Hyland. "All of it or any of it. If there is anything else I can do . . ."

Price looked at the remains of the company. It was scattered around, using the cover that was available, to hide from the Citadel. They were a quiet bunch, unaware that their fate had been sealed by the orders from the fleet.

"I'm going to have to get ready for the big push no matter what," said Hyland.

"I'll let you know what I find out," said Price. He walked off then, glancing up at the Citadel, sitting in the distance. It dominated the whole area, but seemed unconcerned that anyone was close.

He found the radio operator who had set up shop in the shadow of a large boulder. They had stretched a canvas shelter half from the top of the rock to the ground creating a little shade to protect the equipment. Price crouched there, out of the way but in the shade, and tried to think of what to say. He used the code book to compose his analysis of the situation and finally handed it over to the radio operator who broadcast it immediately but there was no response other than the acknowledgment that it had been received.

"When you get an answer, let me know."

"Yes, sir."

Price returned to where Hyland sat. There were a couple of people with her, including Coollege and Monier. Hyland waited until he walked up and said, "I've assembled my assault team."

"Shouldn't it be on a volunteer basis?" asked Price.

"No. You take volunteers when it's a general assignment. You order people when there are special needs. I'm afraid this is going to require special needs."

"What are you planning to do?" asked Price.

"I am going to take seven people and I am going to try to get as close to the Citadel as I can. And then I'm going to retreat and report that we did what we could." She stared at Price for a moment. "I'm taking the officers and not the kids. We know the score but I'm not convinced that all the kids do. We're supposed to take care of them, not use them to test the capabilities of the enemy's fortifications."

"I'll take one of those positions on the assault team," said Price.

"I had counted on that already. You and Coollege and Monier."

"Not Monier," said Price. "She hasn't been in the Army more than a few months. She's one of those kids you were talking about."

"We need her," said Hyland. "She is the key to this thing. If we're going to survive it, we're going to need her."

"I don't see how," said Price.

"Oh, come on . . . She knows things. She can feel things. I don't understand how it works, but I know there are people who can detect danger that the rest of us can't see. I think we need her with us." Hyland stopped talking, realizing that she was preaching to the choir. Price already knew about Monier's abilities.

Price shrugged. "We leave it up to her then. No orders. She has the choice."

"Sure."

"How soon do you take off?" asked Price.

"Sundown."

"Why? There is no reason to wait. The enemy can see as well in the dark as it can in the daylight. Hell, we can see as well in the dark with the image enhancers."

"But we don't have to worry about sunstroke at night," responded Hyland.

The seven soldiers who would make up the assault team met under the canvas tarp next to the big boulder. Swain had volunteered, as had Juan Lopez, a second lieutenant who had been a senior sergeant before receiving his commission, and Pierre

Zouave, the second most senior NCO in the company. Hyland hadn't objected to any of the volunteers because it meant that she didn't have to pick them.

Hyland stood with her back to the Citadel. She didn't want to have to look at it because she believed that she would be dead the moment she reached the point where lasers could target them and the problem would be inherited by her second in command. She was trying to ignore the feelings, telling herself that if it was true, then Monier would know it and would have warned her. To this point Monier had said nothing so she took that as evidence the mission would succeed.

She thought about that for a moment and realized that she was arguing both sides of the question. She had no clue about the future. All she could do was attempt to stack the deck in her favor and hope for the best.

"I don't have much of a plan," said Hyland by way of preamble. "We'll follow standard tactics, that is, use whatever concealment we can find and work our way toward the walls of the Citadel. Once we reach the walls, we'll search for a way to penetrate it." She stopped talking and looked at each of the others. She shrugged and said, "I can't see where there is much of a chance for success, but we have our orders. Anybody have anything to say?"

"We are going under the cover of darkness?" asked Zouave.

"For whatever good it'll do. Captain Price has pointed out that the enemy will have enough advanced equipment that we'll probably show up as plainly as if we were approaching under the noonday sun."

"We could maybe use the heat to mask our approach," said Swain.

Price said, "Actually, once the sun is gone, the lava will be radiating heat back into the atmosphere. That should mask us from infrared. At least early in the evening."

"But there are a hundred other ways to detect us," said Hyland. "Anything we do to hide ourselves, that is, anything we do that upsets the natural balance, might call attention to us. I think our best bet is to move slowly and hope the enemy doesn't view us as a threat because there are so few of us and we are moving so slowly."

"That's the whole plan?" asked Lopez. "Move quietly and not look hostile?"

"Basically," said Hyland. "I'm open to any and all suggestions."

"Well," said Swain, "I would think, if we want to look nonhostile, we should take it all the way. No weapons. Move openly and not search for cover. Just head for it like a walk through the park."

"Oh, for Christ's sake," said Zouave. "This is the most ridiculous thing I have ever heard."

"From now on," said Hyland, "we'll stick to relevant comments." She looked pointedly at Zouave.

"Mine was relevant," said Swain.

"Okay," said Hyland thoughtfully. "I can see that. Move slowly and openly with nothing that looks like a weapon. Maybe a knife but one of those new plastic jobs that the Fleet is trying to palm off on us. Nothing that would give a hostile signature on any of the sensors they must have in there."

"With only good thoughts in our heads," said Price. He wasn't sure if that had been sarcastic or not.

"Something like that," agreed Hyland.

The discussion seemed to die at that point. No one had anything more to say. Hyland looked into each of the faces and wondered what they were thinking. Finally she said, "Everyone grab some chow and sleep. We'll form at 2145 and jump off at 2210. Any questions?"

There were none.

At 2130 hours Hyland walked to the jump-off point, an arbitrary location chosen only because it was in a ravine that was shielded from the Citadel. Monier, dressed in black, with camouflage smeared on her face, was already there. She was sitting with her back to a rock, staring in the direction of the Citadel though she couldn't see it from her position.

"When we move out," she said, "I want you near me at all times. I want to know the instant you pick up anything. Anything at all."

Monier kept her attention focused on the Citadel. "You sure this is a good idea?"

"Hell, it's a lousy idea. It stinks. But there is nothing we can do about it now. We'll reach the damned wall, have our look around, and then get the hell out." Hyland turned and took a long look at the Citadel.

Monier turned so that she could look at Hyland who was little more than a black shape silhouetted against the lava. "Has anyone really thought about what we're going to do if . . . when we get to the wall?"

Hyland sat down and was quiet for a moment. "No," she said. "I've only thought about the best way to get us to the Citadel. That's all I've thought about." She turned to look up toward the Citadel again. "I've been wondering if you can actually communicate . . . mentally, with the people back here. That way we wouldn't have to use the radio. A radio emits detectable radiation."

"What makes you think that any communication worked through me wouldn't be detectable?"

"But I thought . . ."

"Thought waves are detectable and measurable. I don't know if my thought patterns will be significantly different from any others on the enemy equipment or if they have the right equipment to detect them, but they are detectable if someone is looking for them."

"Shit," said Hyland, but there was something there that gave her the germ of an idea. She tried to concentrate, but that forced it deeper, away from her. She let it go, hoping that it would return.

Price strolled up to the ravine, crouched at the edge of it, and said, "I have arrived."

"Not getting here early?" said Hyland.

Price ignored that and said, "How you doing, Rachel?"

She laughed uneasily and said, "Not real good."

Price knew what she was thinking and he didn't have to have any psychic ability to do it. Monier was thinking about the bodies lying out there. They hadn't been able to recover them. It marked the location of engagement. It was the point that the Citadel had decided that the humans would be stopped. It had been the point where the threat had been recognized and eliminated. The Citadel had been ruthlessly efficient with its message. It was telling them to approach no closer. If they attempted it, they would be killed.

"Well," said Price, "all we can do is the best that we can do."

There was a noise and Price looked up to see two of the others straggling in. They were dressed in black and carrying nothing other than canteens and knives. They didn't say much as they dropped down into the ravine.

"I don't like this," Coollege whispered as she passed Price.

Hyland inspected the assembled group, searching the faces for clues about their emotions. Unable to read them easily, she shrugged and said, "I guess it's time. I'll take the point. Let's move slowly, carefully, and try not to look hostile."

"This is stupid," said Lopez.

"Of course," said Hyland, "but we have no choice. We have our orders."

But nobody moved. They sat or stood there, trying to ignore the problem, their orders, and the Citadel. Finally Hyland began to climb from the ravine so she could begin the slow march toward the Citadel.

One by one, the others followed her, stringing out behind her in a long, thin line. No one had ordered them to begin the attack. They had simply fallen in behind the leader.

As they walked, Monier was aware of what the others were feeling now. Those in the squad were all frightened because they didn't understand what they were facing. They knew it was deadly. It had shown them that earlier. But now no one knew if the same rules applied. Maybe, because there were so few of them, they would be able to walk right up to the walls. That was what they hoped.

The minds of the others were filled with confusion . . . confusion and fear. Monier didn't like probing them, but she wanted to know what they really believed. She knew that she felt she would die in the next hour. She wanted to know if the others agreed with that, or if, because of their experience, they believed they would survive.

She reached out then, beyond those around her, to the other squads that were working their way toward the Citadel. Each of them had one or two people who had some psychic ability. Some of them had trained with her in the past. One or two of them was almost as good as she was. She recognized the minds of some them, knew who they were, and what they were thinking. They were as unhappy as she was.

Hyland kept them moving slowly, worming their way around the larger lava boulders, the arroyos, and the ravines. She kept their attention focused on the target. It was nothing more than a black shape looming from the ground in front of them.

They kept moving for an hour and then stopped for a rest. Price wanted to slip down, into one of the shallow depressions close by and hide for a few minutes, but Hyland shook her head. If anyone took a hiding place, that could be interpreted as a hostile act. She wanted them out in the open looking as nonhostile as possible.

Monier said, "Everything is progressing on schedule. Everyone else is fine."

"Keep me informed," said Hyland.

"You get anything," said Price, "I want to know. Anything at all. Especially if you think it's from the interior of the Citadel. Don't try to interpret it, let Coollege and me worry about that."

"Yes, sir."

Hyland stood up and was looking directly at the Citadel, trying to see something more about it. There was a sudden brilliant flash of light, a crisscross of blue beams that looked like a pie wedge of netting that stabbed briefly into the night.

Monier cried out, grabbed her head, and fell to the ground. Price leapt to her. She grabbed his hand, squeezing it tightly. "Someone just died. I felt it. Him. Die."

"The Citadel fired," said Hyland.

Monier waved her hands in the air as if trying to brush away unseen demons. Her breathing was rapid and sweat dampened her forehead. She moaned low in her throat and seemed to lose consciousness for a moment. Then, an instant later she tried to sit up. "I'm all right," she said, pushing aside Price's hands. "I need a minute. Leave me alone."

"What happened?" asked Price.

"I don't know," said Monier, her voice low and quiet. "The Citadel killed them. No warning at all. It just killed them."

"Who?"

"I don't know," said Monier. "One of the other attack squads. I felt them die."

"You all right?" asked Hyland.

Monier rubbed her temples, squeezing her eyes shut. She took a deep breath and checked herself slowly much the way an athlete would after a vicious hit. She made sure that everything was working well and then said, "Yes. Yes, I'm fine."

"We're not going to continue on now, are we?" asked Zouave.

Price looked at the Sergeant and then said to Hyland, "He's right. I don't think we should proceed. Not now."

The idea came to Hyland in a single bright flash. Suddenly she knew what had been bothering her for the last few hours. She looked at Monier and asked, "Can you project?"

Monier didn't answer her right away. Finally she asked, "What do you mean?"

"Can you create images? Can you send those images to others?"

Monier thought about it, nodded, and said, "We have experimented with creating illusions . . . but we need a receptive mind. It's very hard to create images for you to see if that's what you mean."

"Then you might be able to project, at the enemy in the Citadel, the images of us walking toward the Citadel as we sit here and watch."

Monier looked toward Price for help, but said, "I don't know if there is anyone in there to receive."

"But you can do it?"

"Maybe . . . I don't know. It isn't something that we explored with any care . . ."

"Just try it," ordered Hyland. "Try to project an image of us on the move."

"Now?"

"Whenever you feel up to it," said Hyland. She looked at the others and added, "Let's take cover now. Plan A is revised."

CHAPTER

21

Stone, having returned from the mission to bomb the Citadel, and having been carefully debriefed by the Colonel's staff, was alone in the intelligence office on the ship doing the best he could to observe the current activity on the planet's surface. The various sensor arrays, detection equipment, and visual observation gear provided him with an almost unobstructed view of the situation far below them. He wanted to see how the infantry assault, ordered without the benefit of any air support, was progressing. He already knew, based on firsthand observations, how the aerial attack had gone.

On the center screen he had a display that was a computer representation of everything that was happening. It was as if he were looking down on the Citadel from the top. It was a red mass, glowing with a bright light. The infantry positions were marked in green and the assault forces, the few there were, showed in flashing green. The few enemy guns that had been located were marked in orange and there was a bright yellow ring that marked the point where the infantry assault of the afternoon had been stopped with such deadly results.

Stone didn't know exactly where Price and Coollege were, only that they were on the ground with one of the infantry companies. He hoped they were smart enough to stay in the background, away from the action, because that was where the intelligence officers should be. Back where they could observe the action, gather data, and brief the officers who needed the information for the follow-on missions.

There was a quiet chirp behind him and he turned to look toward the hatch. On the display screen mounted on the bulkhead he saw the Colonel. He leaned forward, touched a button, and said, "Please come in, sir." He then killed the display on the center screen because it was classified.

As the hatch irised open, Stone stood and assumed the position of attention.

The Colonel waved a hand and said, "Please be seated." The Colonel found a chair where he could see the main view screen. "What do you have here?"

Stone replaced the display, complete with the top-secret markings on it. He then moved toward the screen, pointed up at it, and began a detailed explanation of everything on the display. He finally looked back at the Colonel and said, "I don't know what's happening now. This is real time, minus about thirty minutes for transmission, interception, and processing. Given our position in space, I can't refine it much better than that."

The Colonel ignored the explanation. Instead, he asked, "You've been thoroughly debriefed by intelligence about the aerial mission?"

"Yes, sir. I'm afraid that there wasn't much I could tell them that they didn't already know."

"What was your impression?"

Stone shrugged and then thought about it carefully. "That the enemy had it, meaning our attack, very well defensed. No wasted motion . . . no wasted shots. They waited until we were in range before they opened fire. That suggests good overall discipline . . . The hardest thing to do is instill proper fire discipline on green troops. They always think you have to throw out rounds to break out the attack. These guys waited until they knew that they could hit something before they shot."

The Colonel, his attention focused on the screen, said, "Very good. You think, then, that we're facing a well-trained force down there."

"Yes, sir. A well-trained and highly disciplined military force."

"Do you think we'll be able to crack the Citadel?"

"Yes, sir. I'm just concerned about the number of people that we'll use up in doing it."

Some of the shapes shifted on the middle screen. There was a sudden flash of light that reached out and touched a number of the infantry troops.

"What's happening?"

Stone said, "The Citadel is now firing on one of the squads. Or rather, it fired about thirty minutes ago."

The beams faded and the lights showing some of the infantry winked out one by one.

"We've lost some people," said Stone quietly.

"Who?"

"I don't know," said Stone.

Monier was sitting up, her back against the rough stone of the lava, feeling the sharp angles pressing into her skin. At the moment she didn't care about that. She was thinking about the deaths she had felt. The sudden blackness that overwhelmed the others.

She didn't want to dwell on that. And she didn't want to look at the Citadel because it had caused those deaths. At the moment the sight of it frightened her badly. She had no idea of what was hidden behind the thick stone walls and that was a situation that she was not used to.

"Anytime you're ready," said Hyland.

Monier shook her head. "I'm sure that I know what I'm doing here. I'm not sure that I'm ever going to be ready again."

"Just try to create the image of us moving through the lava beds toward the Citadel. Think about that and nothing else. See us stand up here, in the arroyo, climb clear, and continue the march."

"I don't know if it'll do any good," said Monier.

"It won't hurt," said Hyland. For an instant she was angry and then it passed. Anger wasn't going to help the situation.

Monier shifted around and then climbed up to where she could see out over the open plain that led to the Citadel. She studied it briefly and then said, "When I begin, please don't talk.

The slightest distraction will break my concentration. I need to concentrate."

"Okay," said Hyland. "Let's spread out and remain alert and stay quiet."

Price stood up so that he could watch the show. The only problem was that there wasn't anything to see. Just the open ground, hidden by the dark and shadows, and the Citadel dominating the landscape beyond it. He looked for some sign that something was happening on the plains near him or inside the Citadel but there was nothing there for him to see. It was as if the Citadel was deserted and the infantry had lifted from the planet.

Price had just about decided that the plan had failed when the blue net flashed again, reaching out to where the phantom squad should be. The laser lights faded as suddenly as they had brightened and that was it. The Citadel took no other notice of them.

"Now what?" asked Price.

"Well . . ."

Coollege said, "Well, we know a couple of things we didn't know before. First, whoever is in there can detect the illusions or whatever created by Monier." She stopped and thought about what she had just said.

"Thought you didn't believe in any of this psychic crap," said Price.

"I do when I can see the evidence with my own eyes. She was obviously creating some kind of image that was detected and then engaged."

"And we know," said Hyland, "that they'll engage anything or anyone who gets too close to them regardless of the steps taken to look nonhostile."

"The question is then," said Price, "will they engage us again?"

"Why wouldn't they?" asked Hyland. "We've seen the evidence."

"Because they've already killed us . . . it would seem inefficient to do it again . . . kill us again," said Price.

"Captain," said Hyland, "I don't believe I care to bet my life on that theory."

"Maybe I can do it again," said Monier. "Make the Citadel think that we've reappeared right where we were detected and eliminated."

"And if," said Coollege, "they're using electronic sensors, they might think they've got a ghost image. They'll fire at it and there'll be no results, they'll stop firing. Then we can walk up."

Price was surprised by the enthusiasm in Coollege's voice. She was never excited about anything, but now she saw a way to penetrate the Citadel and she wanted to take it. Even if it was betting against the odds.

But Hyland seemed to understand what was being said. To Monier, she said, "Do it again. Create another squad and let it take the same route toward the Citadel."

"What good will that . . ." began Monier.

"Just do it, Rachel," said Price. "We'll see if the Citadel will engage the second squad."

"If you think it will do any good . . ." She had realized that as long as they sat in the arroyo, they were safe. If she created phantom squad after phantom squad, she would be in no danger. The danger would come when they were ordered from the arroyo and toward the Citadel.

When they fell silent Monier began to concentrate again. She said nothing. Now all of them were watching the Citadel. But nothing happened this time. There was no burst of fire. Nothing at all.

Monier exhaled explosively and wiped at her face with her hand. Finally she turned to Hyland and said, "I think that's about it."

"You detecting anything from the Citadel?"

"No," said Monier. "I still don't get anything from it."

"Then I guess we try it for real," said Hyland. She turned to the rest of the squad. "Let's saddle up. We've got a long walk to make."

"Wait," said Zouave. "Wait! Let's think about this for a moment."

"Nothing to think about," said Hyland. "We have our orders and no one has rescinded them."

"Which doesn't mean we have to do this stupidly," said Zouave.

"All we have to do is take it easy and let Monier keep her attention focused in case there is any activity," said Price. "It'll be a cakewalk."

"Of course," said Hyland, not sure that she agreed but knowing there was nothing else she could do. "Let's get going."

Within minutes the squad was walking carefully across the broken lava beds, following the path of least resistance, toward the Citadel. Hyland tried to keep the pace steady, but not quick. She sensed a hesitation on the part of Monier who was now on the point. Monier seemed to think she was walking into the muzzle of a rifle. She would do it, but she wasn't going to rush.

As they approached the site where the mass assault had been engaged, where the bodies of the dead soldiers still lay, Hyland said, "Let's hold it up."

Monier shot a glance over her shoulder and then dropped into the closest depression grateful for the reprieve.

Price crawled close to her but this time didn't ask the question that was becoming a standard. He just waited for her answer to it.

Monier answered him anyway. "Nothing."

Hyland joined them and said, "This is really as far as my thinking has taken me. We know, based on the evidence, that the Citadel will fire as we move much farther forward. Unless it views us like it did that second phantom squad."

"Except," said Price, "they've already killed us . . ."

"So you said. Maybe you'd like to test your theory."

Price looked at Hyland and then at Monier. "Rachel?"

"Nothing, Tree. I don't know. I wouldn't want to risk my life on this theory."

Price slipped forward so that he could look at the Citadel. There was nothing to indicate that it was dangerous, but he knew that was meaningless. The evidence of the danger was spread out in front of him.

"No sense in killing off a number of us," said Price. He stood up.

Coollege grabbed his hand. "Don't be stupid, Tree."

"It's not going to fire," he said, not sure that he believed the words. "It's not going to see me as being there."

"Captain," said Monier, "I'm not sure how much faith I would put into this plan."

"There is nothing we can do," said Price, "except test the theory."

Coollege looked at Hyland. "This is your mission."

"And the orders are clear," she said quietly. "We must try to reach the Citadel."

Price stood there, took a deep breath, and said, "I don't believe I want to be buried. Cremated and scattered through space I think would be best. I want my ashes spread through the cosmos by naked virgins."

"That's not funny, Tree," said Coollege. "You're not funny at all."

"Once I'm beyond the ring of bodies, you can join me over there and we can continue to march on to the Citadel."

He wanted to say more but knew that he was just wasting time. He turned and began to pick his way across the lava beds. He reached the line of bodies but didn't stop. He stepped over one and kept his attention focused on the ground so that he wouldn't stumble. Or maybe so that he wouldn't see the flash of laser light.

Then, suddenly, he looked up and realized that he had passed the critical area. The Citadel had not recognized him as a threat and had not engaged him. The question was whether it was because he was alone or because the ruse designed by Monier had fooled them.

He continued on and then stopped. He turned and watched as the rest of the team began to move forward. They fanned out, crossed the ring of dead bodies, and still the Citadel ignored them. With the rest of the squad on the move there was no reason to believe that it was going to engage him now.

As the group joined him, they said nothing. Monier took the point again, followed closely by Swain and Lopez. They strung out again, hoping that if the Citadel opened fire, it would not target all of them at once. That someone would have a chance to get away.

Thirty minutes later they stood at the foot of the Citadel. Price reached out and patted the smooth stone. It was cold. For some reason he had expected it to be warm, maybe from the heat of the sun or maybe from some internal source but it wasn't. It was as cold and seemingly dead as the city that surrounded it.

Monier stood there, looking up toward the top. "Lots of electrical activity," she said. "Nothing else. Just the electricity."

"Now we have to get inside," said Hyland.

"We reached the walls," said Zouave. "We have completed the mission."

Swain ignored him and said, "We could climb." Then he shook his head. "I guess that won't work."

"There has to be something," said Hyland. "Let's spread out and see what we can find."

"What are we looking for?" asked Zouave.

"Maybe water pipes, air ducts, disposal chutes. Hell, maybe we can find a door. I just don't know."

Monier moved to the stone, put both hands on it, palms on the rock. She let the impressions come to her as they did when she held personal objects and photographs. She let her mind go, floating almost above her, and then said, "There seems to be a number of large ducts around the walls about ten feet from the ground."

"Good," said Hyland. "Very good."

In minutes they found one of the openings and were clustered under it. "You know what it is?" asked Hyland.

"No . . . just that it leads into the Citadel. Into the center of it."

"Anything else?" asked Price.

"Only what I've told you. It's really strange but there is nothing but electrical activity."

Hyland asked, "Doesn't that strike you as odd. I mean, if you walked up to a fleet installation of this size wouldn't you pick up something?"

"It would be screaming at me," said Monier. "But this is an alien site. What would happen on Earth, or in our fleet, just doesn't matter here."

"So what do you want to do, Captain?" asked Swain.

"Follow our orders and penetrate this," said Hyland.

Swain put his hands together to make a step to lift her up, toward the opening. "After you, Captain."

She put her foot in Swain's hand, stretched out until she could grab the lip of the opening, and said, "Thanks." She then began to haul herself up.

• • •

"Somebody reached the walls of the Citadel," said Stone.

The Colonel turned his attention to the main view screen. "Who is it?"

"I'm not sure, sir. It's only seven people. I don't know how they did it. The other teams were either engaged and killed or turned back."

"Not much that seven people can do," said the Colonel.

"They did get in," said Stone. "That's more than anyone else was able to do."

"Well, I suppose I'd better get back to the command post. This might be the break that we need."

"You think they'll be able to tell us anything?"

"I don't know about that, but we've got them in. Now we'd better be ready to follow up."

"Yes, sir."

The Colonel stood up and moved to the hatch. "You're ready for another flight?"

"If necessary," said Stone.

The hatch irised open and the Colonel disappeared through it. Stone watched him go and wondered what he was thinking about. The last aerial assault had been a disaster.

CHAPTER

22

Once Hyland was inside the opening, she took a moment to look around but there was nothing in it of interest. It was a long, narrow tube. She couldn't stand upright in it, but she could stand. There was a light, cool breeze coming from the interior and the almost indetectable odor of ozone. She thought of it as the smell of electricity.

She crouched down and turned, looking back out onto the lava bed. She reached a hand out, as if she expected to haul one of the others up to join her inside. "Come on," she said. "Let's go."

Swain was still standing at the base of the wall, looking up at her. "What did you find?"

"Tunnel. Come on."

"Captain," said Swain, "I think we should get out of here now." He turned and looked at Price for support of his opinion. "Tell her, sir."

But Price wasn't interested in getting out of there now. He was looking at the opening and Hyland. He knew what she was thinking. They had reached the Citadel. They were standing next to the wall with a way to penetrate to the interior of it. They had to proceed. It was an opportunity they couldn't pass up. The intelligence value of the mission was unprecedented. Besides, he had to know what was inside it.

"If you're not going," said Price, "then stand aside. I will."

"Sir . . ."

Coollege was next to him. "Maybe we should think about this, Tree."

"Put you hands together and give me a boost," said Price. He made it clear that he was issuing an order. "Monier, you have to come inside with us. The rest can stay out here as a rear guard."

"I'm going with you," said Coollege.

Price put his hands together and said, "Then let's do it. Sergeant Swain, you are the rear guard. You will stay here with the remainder of the force and wait for us. You will let no one in behind us."

"Yes, sir." The relief in his voice was unmistakable.

Price helped Coollege and then Monier up into the opening. Then, with Swain's help, he climbed up. Once inside, he sat back against the rough stone of the wall and listened, but the only sounds were the quiet rustling caused by the air flowing past him and a low hum that might have been distant machinery.

"I've only gone about fifty, sixty feet down here," said Hyland. "I don't see any problems."

"Except that it's pitch-black and we have no sources of light."

"So we move carefully so that we don't walk off a ledge," said Hyland. "I'll take the point. Monier, you're right behind me."

"And I'll bring up the rear," said Price.

"What about the others?" asked Hyland.

"Posted as a rear guard."

"I wish you'd have let me do that, Captain," said Hyland. "Those are my people."

"Sorry. You can countermand my orders if you think it necessary."

"No, you're probably right."

With that they began to work their way deeper into the Citadel. Hyland was moving slowly, checking the footing carefully before she trusted the floor. In the distance was a shimmer of light. She had the impression of a large, domed area, but that was only an impression. She worked her way toward it slowly, stopped to let the others catch her, and then started forward again.

They reached an area where a light-producing lichen grew. The light was dull and green and did very little to illuminate the tunnel, but it did make it possible to see the floor under them. They could move faster even if the light was poor.

But after twenty minutes of walking hunched over, Hyland's back ached. She called a halt and slipped to the floor, leaning against the rough stone of the tunnel. She wiped a hand over her face and rubbed her eyes. She turned her attention to Monier. "Any signs of life?"

"No. Nothing."

Coollege said, "How do we know that there's anyone in here?"

"Because we've always assumed . . ." Hyland stopped talking abruptly, realizing that there had never been a single shred of evidence that suggested biological life existed inside the Citadel. The important word was *assumed*. There had to be a sentient creature at the center of the Citadel because a computer program, no matter how sophisticated, couldn't respond to every single threat thrown at it. Computer programs couldn't think for themselves. They could come very close but they were never self-aware and that was why there had to be someone, something alive in the Citadel.

"What about it?" asked Price.

Monier didn't respond. Instead she turned and placed her hands on the rough stone and let her mind go blank. When she had drained her mind, she let the impressions and feelings wash over her, probing with her mind, searching for anything. She felt the impressions build, but they weren't from the present. They were from somewhere in time, somewhere in the past . . . from the workers who had built the Citadel a long time before.

These were alien minds that didn't seem to relate to the beings she had seen as they had crossed the planet's surface. She didn't understand all of it but she could catch some when it was raw emotion. Words floated up to her. Strange words that had no meaning for her. But she could understand the fear of those forced to build the Citadel. Or the hate. Hate directed to something unseen but powerful enough to compel them to construct the Citadel. The deaths of the workers didn't slow the progress. No time was allowed to mourn the dead. They were covered over, dragged out, or incorporated into the structure. The only clear thing was that the construction workers were not from the same race that was forcing the construction.

She tried to reach out, beyond that tunnel, beyond the closest chambers, and deeper, into the center of the Citadel, looking for something alive. But she could find nothing. It was as if she were inside a giant computer. She could feel the electricity around her but nothing that came from a living, breathing creature.

Probing deeper, she began to feel things, feel the workings of the machine itself. She began to get impressions but nothing she could define. Then the only thing she knew was that there was nothing alive in the Citadel now other than the people with her.

She shook herself, as if to throw off the thoughts, and said, "There's nothing in here."

"Then we get the hell out," said Coollege.

Hyland didn't say anything for a moment. "I think we should press on now that we've managed to get in. Captain?"

"I'd have to agree," said Price. "The enemy might, at any moment, realize their mistake. What worked once might not work again." He hadn't understood that Monier was telling them that there was nothing alive in the Citadel.

"And now that we're in," said Hyland, "maybe we should try to destroy it."

"With what?" asked Monier. "We have no weapons . . . no tools."

"Then we can test the principle that there are no dangerous weapons, just dangerous men and women."

"Shit," said Coollege.

"Aren't you listening to me?" asked Monier. "I said that there is nothing in here that is alive. Nothing."

"There has to be," said Price. "You're just not getting it . . . reading it."

Coollege said, "You have a nasty habit of ignoring that which you don't want to hear. Tree, she said there is *nothing in here.*"

"Someone . . . something is controlling this thing," he said. "We've got to locate it."

"I agree," said Hyland. "I've lost too many people to let this opportunity escape us. We have to go deeper."

"Rachel?" asked Price.

Monier didn't respond. She twisted around so that she was on her hands and knees. She crawled forward and said, "I think that I should lead the way."

"You have the point," said Hyland, agreeing with her.

Monier crawled forward more rapidly, came to a branch, and reached out with her mind. She put a hand into the left tunnel and then selected the right. Over her shoulder, she said, "The left is a trap . . . a deadfall."

Price stopped and said, "A booby trap?"

Monier let out a low moan and fell forward.

Hyland scrambled to her. "What the hell is happening?"

In a voice tinged with fear, she said, "The others are dead."

"Dead! What do you mean dead?"

"They have been killed."

"All of them?"

"Except Swain . . . He was sticking close to the wall. The others had drifted away from it . . . It killed them."

"That means we're stuck," said Coollege.

"That means," said Price, "that we now have no choice but to push on."

Hyland waved a hand. "Shut up and let me think." After a few minutes, she asked Monier, "Have you noticed any change in the activity in here?"

"No."

"Okay . . . okay, that suggests they may have tripped some kind of automatic defense. The deadfall you mentioned suggests there are booby traps. There are defenses that are independent of the main body of the Citadel."

"Great," said Coollege. "Maybe now it's time to get the hell out of here."

"No!" snapped Hyland. "We've come too far to give it up. We press on."

"Now?" asked Monier.

Hyland heard the strain in her voice and said, "No. We take a break first."

The Colonel stood in front of the assembled pilots and said, "We have managed to penetrate the Citadel. We have a team who is inside it right now."

For an instant no one said a word and then the room burst into applause. The pilots shouted and slapped each other on the back. It was as if they had scored the winning touchdown or hit the winning home run. They thought they had just been told that all follow-on missions would be scrubbed.

The Colonel stood quietly and watched them. One by one they fell silent and when the room was quiet again, he said, "Unfortunately, I'm not sure how to exploit this. We have a team inside the Citadel, but they don't have the equipment or the manpower to destroy it from the inside."

"We're not going to let this opportunity slip through our fingers?" asked one of the pilots. The instant the words were out of his mouth, he regretted them.

"No," said the Colonel. "No, we're not. But we're not going to attack without some thought either. We all know how well the Citadel fought off the last aerial assault."

"But now we have people on the inside. If they could disrupt the flow of . . ."

The Colonel focused his gaze on the man. "I'm aware of the problems, Lieutenant."

Stone leaned back in his chair and looked at the porthole. There was a broad field of stars and the disk of a planet several hundred thousand miles away. Somewhere on the planet's surface was the Citadel.

With people on the inside, to create trouble, it made sense to launch another aerial assault that might be able to exploit their advantage. If they could coordinate it properly.

"At the moment," said the Colonel, "we don't know what is happening inside the Citadel. We know that a few of our people are in there. I want to be in a position to respond to any opportunity."

Stone grinned to himself. It meant that they were going to flood the sky with attack ships and if anything happened in the Citadel, they would be ordered in. Those who thought, only moments before, that they were safe now realized that they were wrong.

"Flight commanders will have a schedule for patrol. This will be a maximum effort operation. All ships, pilots, and crews will be used. There will be little time for rest during the next twenty-four hours. We will be on a full rotation for that time. You'll have to catch what rest you can when you can. Eat when you have the chance."

"Rules of engagement?" asked one of the pilots.

"We will fire when fired upon. You will not initiate an attack unless ordered to do so. We must try to coordinate with the people inside the Citadel." The Colonel fell silent and looked into the grim faces of the men and women inside the briefing room. "Are there any questions?"

Of course there were none. Everyone understood exactly what had to be done.

They probed deeper, out of communication with the rest of the company back beyond the ring of dead troopers and with the fleet far overhead. They were on their own, as far as they knew, searching for the answers that would end the problems created by the Citadel.

The interior of the tunnel got lighter as they pushed in deeper. The fungus was growing thicker but it was never very bright. From deeper, farther inside the Citadel came a dull pounding, suggesting the workings of the internal machinery. And there was an overwhelming surge of electrical energy. Monier felt it smashing into her, blanking out the impressions she was receiving from the Citadel's rock and stone outer walls.

Hyland caught her and asked, "Are we getting close?"

"Close to what?" asked Monier. She had to concentrate on the words to understand them. The air felt as if it were charged with enough power to light a bulb.

"The source of the power?"

"I don't know. I can't tell."

"Shit," said Coollege. "This is doing no good."

"Shut up," said Price.

Monier sat back and leaned against the stone. She rubbed her temples. "There is nothing around us. No beings of any kind. There were once, but no more. They programmed this thing to take care of itself just as they programmed the ship to be independent of communication with them."

"So maybe this part of the Citadel is storage?" said Coollege.

"No," said Monier, "you don't understand. Long ago there

was someone in here . . . very long ago, but no more. There is nothing here."

"Storage," repeated Coollege.

"No."

"If it is empty," said Price, "it might be easy to sabotage this section of it."

"How?" asked Hyland. "I haven't seen any wires to yank out or printed circuits to smash. Nothing but this stone tunnel that seems to lead nowhere."

"So what do we do?" asked Monier.

"I think we move a little deeper into this thing and see if there isn't something we can do to break it."

"You sure that there is no one in here?" asked Price.

"Yes, sir. It's empty."

"That makes this a giant computer?" asked Coollege. "A system that someone left on when they abandoned the planet?"

"It's not abandoned," said Price, thinking of the creatures they had seen putting in the pipeline. Then he understood it all. They were the maintenance team, grown to keep the Citadel functioning, just as the little alien had been on the asteroid to keep it functioning. Sometimes there was nothing better for a chore than a flesh and blood hand. The Citadel grew the creatures to perform those tasks that it couldn't do for itself.

In that moment he understood the true nature of the evil that they faced. Not an alien race but an alien machine that recognized nothing but its own existence. Everything was created to serve it. The machine had bypassed humanity and become a god. The universe existed for it.

CHAPTER
23

They arrived at a large, internal area that was filled with machinery that no one recognized. There were glowing lights on the fronts of some of them. A couple of large machines seemed to be hovering in the air, inches off the stone floor. None of them were connected to anything yet they all pulsated with energy. The air was charged with electricity, and each of them felt the hair on their bodies stirring.

"Well," said Coollege, "we finally found something." She wasn't sure that she was thrilled.

Price dropped from the tunnel to the floor of the chamber about eight feet below. He walked forward slowly, thinking that the machinery reminded him, vaguely, of those they had found on the asteroid.

"Now we sabotage this thing," said Hyland.

"Without tools?" asked Coollege.

"We were without tools on the asteroid," said Price, "we did more than just sabotage equipment. We know more here than we did then. We can wreck all this."

"Shut up and listen," said Hyland. "We don't need tools and we don't need to wreck anything." She knelt near Monier and asked, "Can you tell me anything about this thing?"

"No. I just can't get anything."

"I mean," said Hyland, "how many parts are there. How much backup? How big is it?"

"I don't really . . ." Monier said but reached out with a hand, as if to touch one of the free-standing machines. She searched for a pattern in all the electrical activity. She sensed an immenseness that was frightening. The machine filled the entire Citadel. Each part of it had a backup to a backup to a backup that was all backed up. It was redundancy to the extreme.

"Is there anything that you can do?" asked Hyland.

Monier sat down and rubbed her thighs as if to dry the palms of her hands on her uniform. She took a deep breath and remembered one of the exercises. They had been able, with thought waves, to erase the hard drive and bubble memories in small computers. The task hadn't been difficult when it had been explained and demonstrated to her. But she had never tried anything as large and complex as the mainframe on the ship, let alone anything like the Citadel.

"What are you going to do to it?"

Monier shrugged and then the answer came to her. It was right out of the exercises from Earth. "Convince one part of it that another is beginning to malfunction. Force it to run diagnostics taking up more of the capabilities. Cause it to slip and make errors and erase part of its memory. Convince it that part of it is breaking down and destroying itself."

"That'll work?"

"Who knows. If it does, we can force part of it to shut down and that reduces the task. We have to view it as a series of small steps."

"What can we do to help?" asked Hyland.

Monier pointed at the machines. "Smash those."

Price grinned and turned, grabbing the front of one of the machines. He worked his fingernails under its cover and pulled. The door opened easily, showing the interior of it. Clear plastic and blinking lights that seemed to have no real function. Price reached in, grabbed, and pulled. A panel came free and Price threw it to the floor. It didn't break.

But that didn't stop him. He pulled other components out, tossing them aside. Coollege joined him, ripping the front from another of the machines and stripping the components from them. She stomped on a pile of them but they still didn't break.

Monier watched for a moment and then closed her eyes so that she could concentrate. At first she thought about trying to fool the machine into thinking it was breaking down, but then decided against that. Instead, she wondered if she could create a fleet of phantom ships to attack in much the same way that she had created the phantom squad earlier.

Price had torn the front from the last of the machines. He'd pulled the first of the clear plastic boards from it to disable it. Now there was nothing else for them to do. Price didn't think they'd done much damage.

Monier wasn't aware of that. She was thinking of a huge fleet. First it had just been the fighters dropping in from space. Then she'd thought about it and realized that a phantom fleet could contain anything that she could dream up. Hundreds of ships. Thousands of them. And she knew already that the Citadel would register her impressions. That had been proven earlier when it attacked her phantom squad.

On the ground, outside, the soldiers who ringed the Citadel saw a sudden burst of firing from it but they saw no overhead threat. The fleet that Monier envisioned was only visible on the sensors of the computers in the Citadel. In orbit, the Colonel's staff noticed the sudden increase in activity but didn't know what it meant. The consensus was that the Citadel was engaging in a "mad minute" when everyone got the opportunity to fire his or her weapon to make sure that it worked.

Monier was aware of the electrical activity around her. It was slowly dropping off as the Citadel began to understand the nature of the threat. With no results from its weapons and no evidence of damage to it, it began to deactivate some of its weapons.

Monier realized it. The electrical activity was falling away so she began to create hot spots. She thought that she might be able to convince the Citadel to shut down some of its systems if it believed that they were about to be damaged by heat. She sensed where they would be the most effective and kept at it until the electrical activity decreased near it. Then she shifted her attention to another area. If the Citadel tried to reactivate a system, she hit it again. She wanted it to believe that it was too hot to function.

Stone, in the intell office, watched the activity on the Citadel and suddenly realized that he was looking at the solution. Someone had gotten into the Citadel and was creating a problem for it, internal sabotage. If the Citadel was firing at empty space, it meant the sensors and equipment were fouled and that could be the answer for them.

He hit the intership communications and said, "Colonel, I think it's time to launch everything."

There was an instant's hesitation and the Colonel said, "You have something?"

"The Citadel is firing all its weapons."

There was no response from the Colonel. Instead a Klaxon began to sound. The Colonel was scrambling the flight crews. They were going to attack the Citadel immediately.

Stone ran from the intell office, down the corridor, and to the flight bay. He ran across the deck to his ship and opened the hatch. He pulled himself up into the cockpit and flipped on the switches. He ran through the run-up quickly. He pulled the shoulder harness around, buckled himself in, and announced to flight control that he was ready to roll.

"Roger, Four," said flight control. "Stand by."

Monier tried to figure out what would be the most disastrous thing to happen to the Citadel. What would it fear more than anything, if it could feel fear of anything. And then she had it.

She created a single large ship that hovered above the Citadel, positioning it to drop a gigantic bomb. She created the bomb bay that opened slowly and let it release the single weapon it carried. She let it fall slowly, ignoring the force of gravity. The Citadel brought a series of weapons to bear, but the bomb kept falling, almost as if the weapons weren't shooting at it. Abruptly the Citadel stopped shooting because it had determined that the bomb would miss the outer wall by more than one hundred feet. Although the Citadel believed that the weapon would be thermonuclear, it calculated that it would survive the blast created by the weapon.

But the bomb didn't detonate at the optimum altitude as expected. It didn't detonate at ground level. It penetrated the ground, sinking into the soil as if it were so much water. When it reached a thousand feet below the surface, Monier created a minor blast and then a secondary that shook the ground around it, sending seismic shocks through the planet. They seemed to reflect from the core of the planet, echoing toward the mantle. She remembered the vast lava plain on which the Citadel sat. It was not unrealistic to believe that a volcanic eruption could be triggered by a well-placed nuclear device.

Stone followed the flight leader out of the bay and pushed the throttle forward as he tried to keep up. There was a bright blast of light from the rear of the flight leader's ship. Stone followed as it dove to the right, racing toward the planet's surface. There was no maneuvering to disguise their route. They dropped from the fleet and headed toward the planet by the quickest route possible.

On the radar he could see the fighters strung out behind him. A hundred ships launched from four different fleet carriers. They were joining into a single formation under the control of an officer who was coordinating from one of the fleet ships.

Stone was the number two man in the formation. Only his flight leader who had taken off before him was in front of him. He didn't have to worry about the other ships, only the one in front of him.

The planet changed from an indistinct disk with little detail visible to the naked eye to a large planet that filled the small cockpit window. Through an obscuring cloud layer the top of the world where the Citadel stood on the black plain was visible. The flashing of the laser cannon and the strobbing of the smaller weapons suggested that it was not wise to attack at the moment.

But they ignored that. The mission was clear. Hit the Citadel with a barrage of weapons. They fell out of the sky in a long line and formed on a broad front to attack the Citadel all at once. Stone pulled even with the flight leader, only a few feet to his right and slightly behind him.

Some of the weapons on the Citadel were directed at them, but more of them flashed past them, ineffectively targeting empty space. Stone's flight leader launched every missile that he carried and dropped all the bombs. He salvoed the weapons, giving the Citadel as many new targets as he could before he pulled up to fly over the top of the target.

Stone reached down and flipped the selector to salvo and did the same. Fourteen missiles were launched, directed at the Citadel in general but no specific spot on it. He dropped all the bombs he carried, letting them drift down toward the Citadel to detonate on the walls.

As he pulled up and away, he twisted around and looked back. No weapons had been fired at him. His ship hadn't been touched. Now his weapons were beginning to impact on the surface of the Citadel, tiny, bright flashes of lights as the bombs and missiles penetrated the defensive systems and shields that tried to protect the Citadel.

"We hit it," he shouted over the radio. "Slam-dunked it."

A minute later the flight controller said, "No unnecessary chatter."

But that did nothing to stop Stone. He was watching the attack on the center screen on his instrument panel using the rear-looking camera. The Citadel was taking hits . . . finally.

Monier had a feeling for what was happening on the top surface of the Citadel. She kept trying to create mental hot spots in the Citadel and to convince it and its sensors that something was happening to it. She could also create new ships out of the air to confuse the targeting systems in the Citadel. But she was too busy to tell anyone with her what she felt and what she believed was happening. She could only sit there, concentrating and trying to sense what was happening as she created as much trouble as possible for the Citadel.

All the troops, whether on the ground or in space, watched the fireworks with growing fascination. They watched as their ships fell out of the night sky, made a single pass, and then rocketed upward, disappearing in seconds. The light show was impressive, the colors extraordinary. There was a laser net over the Citadel but it couldn't stop the fighters or the weapons. They danced and flashed and strobbed, but the weapons still penetrated, hitting the top and sides of the Citadel, caving in parts of it.

Inside the Citadel the situation was growing worse. Hot spots were exploding all over the interior, but now only a few of them were caused by Monier. It sensed the shaking deep underground from the planet-busting weapon that Monier had imaged. It was shutting more and more of itself down, trying to protect the delicate internal circuits. The threat was too great. The danger was too great.

Monier kept pressing the advantage. She kept shifting the hot spots and creating the shaking of the ground. Now she began to think about a volcanic eruption. She tried to convince the sensors that the surface of the Citadel was superheating as magma bubbled to the surface.

The Citadel could no longer cope with all the threats . . . not the threats from space that seemed to drop out of nowhere to attack it . . . not the threats of the heating of its internal components . . . and not the threats of the coming volcanic eruption. It felt itself being destroyed by forces that only hours ago it had swept from the skies and the ground around it. Now those forces, aided by nature, were about to overwhelm it.

Outside the Citadel, the soldiers were applauding the light show and were disappointed when it suddenly ended. One second there seemed to be thousands of brightly colored beams crisscrossing in space and the next there was nothing except the fading images on their retinas.

There were a few minor explosions on the top of the Citadel that were hidden by the distance. Smoke arose from a number of fires, but the exciting light display was gone. The Citadel had given up.

Monier suddenly sat straight up and said, in a surprised voice, "It's dead."

"What do you mean dead?" asked Price.

"I feel no more electrical activity. The electricity is gone."

"What's happening?" asked Hyland.

"It's over. It's shut down. We've killed it. There is nothing left but the stone."

"You mean we beat it?" asked Coollege.

"Yes," said Monier, her voice rising. "Yes. We beat it. We own it."

For a moment longer they sat quietly, digesting what they had heard. Then Hyland stood up and said, "I think we'd better get out of here."

Price reached back, holding out a hand for Monier. "Come on, Rachel."

Coollege said, "I don't believe this . . . it seemed so easy."

"Easy?" asked Hyland. "There are a lot of dead men and women who would disagree with you."

"Yeah," said Coollege.

With that Price lifted himself into the tunnel and turned to help the others climb up. They began the journey out of the Citadel.

CHAPTER

24

Randly Clark had dropped back into space flying his scout ship, rather than a fighter. He had replaced the holo and video, had new books, and a food supply that was fit for the General's mess. He was as happy as he could be. There was no responsibility for others, no morning rituals that had to be followed, and no formations for him to stand.

He thought about the mission he'd led on the Citadel, thought about the men and women who had died, and then told himself that it wasn't his fault. It was the fault of the brass hats who thought they could attack the Citadel and not suffer any consequences.

He told himself that frequently, but the scenes over the planet as the ships with him had exploded were never far from his mind. He'd go an hour or two without thinking about it and then it would bubble up making him slightly sick to his stomach. And he would tell himself again that it wasn't his fault.

So now, out in space once more away from the fleet and the responsibilities, he tried to convince himself that life would go back to the way it was. Sometimes he believed that. Until the screams woke him and he knew that people had relied on him and that he'd failed them.

In a matter of minutes Randly Clark's life had changed and he was fighting to put it back. He knew that it would take time, but he also knew that he would succeed. Eventually.

The fact that she had gotten the medal bothered her greatly. She had done nothing other than her duty and then the Colonel had handed her a medal. Susan Hyland sat in her office, her feet up, holding the small box with the medal in it. She opened the lid, looked at the scrap of colored cloth and a bit of bright metal. It reflected the sacrifice of about half her company. A lot of people had died so that she could earn the medal.

Sergeant Swain entered the ship's office, saw her holding the box, and asked, "Is that it?"

"Yeah. That's it. The Colonel gave it to me this morning. Formal ceremony will be in about a week."

"Well, you deserved it," said Swain.

"No . . . Monier deserved it. Price and Coollege deserved it because they didn't have to be there . . ."

"That's the way it is, Captain. The leader gets the medal and the rest of us get nothing."

Hyland grinned and hit a key on the computer. The screen brightened. She pointed to it and said, "The one real advantage of being in command is that I can make your life miserable too. Take a look at that."

Swain moved around and saw his name at the top of the screen. It was the standard form used for promotion. He was to be commissioned as a second lieutenant.

"No, ma'am, I don't think this is a good idea."

"I lost too many officers on that mission. I need replacements whom I can trust. You win. Sorry, Lieutenant. The order goes into effect tomorrow morning. I would suggest you have your last fling with the NCOs because tomorrow they won't speak to you."

Swain stood silently for a moment and then nodded. "Thank you," he said. "I appreciate the confidence you have in me."

"You're welcome, Lieutenant."

Price sat in the intell office, all the display screens showing aspects of the Citadel and the assault on it or what had been found inside it. Hundreds of technicians had been given the opportunity to explore it. They had been landed on the top when the fires had burned out and they had found their way down into it.

Of course, that was after the soldiers had cleared it. They had moved through every level exploring it fully. They had found no living beings in the Citadel just as Monier had said. They had found no bodies either. It was simply a giant computer, self-aware to a degree, that ran the planet, using the few biological creatures it allowed to exist as its hands and fingers.

It was the strangest enemy that Price had ever seen. It was almost as if the war had been fought against a giant video game where you didn't lose your coin but your life.

Coollege entered the office, dropped into one of the chairs, and asked, "What the hell is going on now?"

"Review," said Price. "Have to tell the Colonel all that we know."

Coollege twisted around so that she was looking at him. "Guess I was wrong about Monier. She came in handy. She could do what she said she could."

"Yeah."

"I'm really sorry about my attitude," said Coollege. "It was unprofessional of me."

"That it was," said Price, "but it's over now. Forget it."

She nodded and asked, "They figure out who built the Citadel?"

"Technically it built itself," said Price. "Developed the laborers through genetic engineering and designed itself. Once it was completed, it let the creatures die off." Price laughed. "It did create the asteroid for space exploration. There are probably a hundred more of those things out there. That seems to be what the technicians have determined so far."

"So what happens now?" asked Coollege.

Price shrugged. "I don't know. But I do know that this is over."

She looked at the screen and watched the information as it paraded across it. She knew that they would be expected to analyze it and then prepare a major report that would be filed away in the mainframe. She had the horrible thought that the mainframe might take the report and use it to create a life for itself. Then she laughed at that. It was the stuff of alien planets and science fiction novels.

"You had breakfast?" she asked.

Price took a deep breath and rocked back in his seat. There was enough work there to keep them, and Stone, and Monier, busy for the next several months. He wouldn't be able to do anything right away.

"Nope," he said. "I was hoping we could eat together."

Standing up, she said, "I thought you'd never ask."